A LIFETIME OF LOVE

A WEDDING, A FAMILY CRISIS, AND A SECRET DREAM

CARMEN KLASSEN

ETA Publishing Ltd

ALSO BY CARMEN KLASSEN

SUCCESS ON HER TERMS SERIES

* * *

NON-FICTION TITLES

CONTENTS

PART I

CHAPTER 1

"Oh, Jaz. It's magical!" Carrie slowly turned to one side and then the other, as if moving too fast would break the spell she was under. Her wedding dress—custom designed by Jasmine Lee, owner and designer of the Jazzy Clothing Company—was beyond perfect.

The bodice fit her with no room to spare, and yet it felt like she could do anything in it. Over the shimmering white satin, the softest chiffon Carrie had ever touched followed the off-the-shoulder silhouette, wrapping around her arms in a narrow band.

The chiffon was delicately overlaid on the fitted skirt, so it clung to the skirt and floated at the same time. She felt like a modern day princess. Carrie continued to slowly turn around until she saw the long slit at the back of the skirt.

"Whoa! That's quite the slit!"

"It is OK? I can change anything you want!" Jaz was standing behind Carrie in tailored black dress pants with a white long-sleeved blouse that had an asymmetrical collar. She looked nervously at Carrie.

"Hey, if I can't look stunning on my wedding day, I give up! No, don't change a thing. This dress, I mean, wow! It's nothing like I could have imagined, but wearing it makes me feel like the luckiest bride in the world." She reached over and hugged her friend. "Thank you!" she whispered.

"Oh good! I'm so glad you like it! Holy cow, you're getting married in two weeks! Can you even believe it?"

"Sometimes it feels like Jonathan and I have always been together. And then other times I have trouble believing that any of this is true!"

A little voice called from another room.

"That's Alex done with his nap! Here, let me unzip you and then you can get dressed. Just put the dress on the chair here."

Carrie paused for a minute as Jaz walked out and closed the door behind her. She couldn't help feeling a bit of motherly pride for the teenager who had come so far since showing up on her doorstep, homeless and pregnant last year.

Just as she was pulling a cable-knit sweater over her t-shirt, her phone rang. Seeing Kara's name pop up, she quickly answered. Why would Kara be calling her from the clinic?

"Hey Kara!"

"Carrie, we're having a bit of a crisis with one of your clients. I know it's outside your contract, but could you possibly come to the clinic right away? I tried to get a hold of Dr. Henshaw, but there's no answer. It's urgent."

"Yes, of course. I can be there in ten minutes." She quickly put her phone back in her purse, checked that she was dressed and hadn't forgotten anything, then popped her head into Jaz's bedroom. "Something's come up with one of my clients and I need to rush to the clinic. I'll catch up later."

Jaz looked up from the changing table where Alex's kicking feet

4

were visible, "OK. Hope it works out. Let me know if you need anything from us."

Thoughts of her wedding vanished as she rushed to her car. She hoped that whatever it was, it was something she could help with. It would be much worse if it was a situation she couldn't do anything about.

Carrie quickly entered the clinic and went to the reception area. The receptionist waved around to the back, and Kara came out of a room with a strange sound coming from it.

"Hey, how can I help?"

"Well, I'm not sure you can. If at any point you think this is beyond you, we'll call an ambulance. The short version is that Megan's in there with her mom, who's having some kind of breakdown."

"Megan, the 14-year-old I've been seeing?" Carrie tried to put Megan's story together and understand what might be going on. Megan struggled with a learning disability and a tendency to skip school as a coping strategy. Carrie didn't know about anything else at this point, but they only had two sessions together so far.

"Yep. She came in here and said her mom was in the car freaking out. We got her into a room, but I couldn't understand a thing she was saying."

"No problem. I'll see what I can do." Taking a deep breath, Carrie opened the door and stepped into the room, quickly closing the door behind her. The sound was coming from a woman who looked to be in her forties, wearing gray sweatpants and a faded green t-shirt. Her blond hair was in a messy ponytail, and her hands covered her face as she rocked back and forth. A sort of moaning sound seemed to come from her.

Beside her, Megan sat looking at the floor, her eyes wide and ringed by dark circles that stood out on her pale face. Her dark hair was in a French braid, and she wore a cream hoodie with blue jeans and black ankle boots.

It didn't look like Carrie would get any response out of the mom, so she turned to Megan with a soft smile. "Hi Megan! I'm happy to see you again, although it seems like you're having some challenges. What can you tell me?"

Megan angled her head towards her mom and raised her eyebrows. Guessing that she wanted Carrie to address her mom, Carrie continued, "We'll give your mom some time for now. I want to focus on you."

The sound seemed to fade slightly, before beginning with even more force. Carrie pulled her chair closer to Megan so she could hear her better.

"My mom was talking to me this morning about this boy in our apartment who's always trying to start something with me. She kept trying to make me say I'd go out with him, and I got mad and told her I didn't like boys."

Carrie waited for almost a minute. "OK, what happened next?"

"She asked me if I was gay, and I said 'maybe'. Then she just went to the couch and started doing this and didn't stop. After a while I got scared that she was having, like, a breakdown or something. It was loud, and I thought the neighbors might hear and call the cops. But I didn't want to take her to the hospital in case they locked her up. So I kinda dragged her to the car and drove to the clinic. I thought maybe you could help her—us."

"Wait a minute. *You* drove here?"

"Oh, um... only because it was an emergency."

Carrie remembered Megan saying something about how her mom needed a lot of help with 'things'. She wished she had stopped to read the notes from their last session before entering the room. But she'd have to deal with the issue of a minor driving a car later.

"How are you doing?" she asked, lowering her voice slightly.

"Me? But I'm here for my mom."

"Right now your mom hasn't given me any sign she wants to talk. Whenever she does, I'm here for her too." Carrie reached over and put her hand gently on Megan's arm. "How are you?"

"I don't know. I wish there was no such thing as dating. It's so confusing. I'm trying to work on the stuff you've been teaching me, but I can't handle all this other stuff at the same time."

The sounds coming from Megan's mom were already becoming quieter. As they did, Carrie continued to lower her voice.

"Tell me about the stuff you're working on." She wanted to take the focus off Megan's mom, and hoped Megan would follow her lead.

"Um, I've been trying to be more responsible for me, and thinking about how to take care of myself at school instead of trying to figure out what other people think I should do."

"That's fantastic! Have you been to school this week?"

Megan sat up a bit, "Yeah, I went after our session on Wednesday, and all day yesterday."

"Megan, congratulations! That's a huge accomplishment!" Carrie saw movement out of the corner of her eye, but kept her focus on Megan. "And did you think about what we talked about on Wednesday?"

"You mean how my thoughts are a choice? Like, the worry thoughts?" Carrie nodded and Megan continued, "Most of the time I don't really think about... about thinking. But when I did stop and ask what I was thinking, it seemed like my thoughts were pretty messed up. Like only thinking about bad stuff. So then I'd try to say, 'I love myself' like you said to do and then I'd try to think about good things that I know are real."

"That's a lot of progress to make on something that can be challenging to change!"

"I think maybe that's why I told my mom that stuff this morning. I wanna be, like, true to me. You know? Not just pretending to be what other people want? I mean, I don't know if I'm gay, I just don't know if I'm *not* gay."

The sounds from Megan's mom had completely stopped.

"Tell me, what do you have control over right now?"

"What I think, what I say, and what I do."

Carrie gave her a thumbs up, "And what do you *not* have control over?"

Megan glanced at her mom and then quickly looked away. "Pretty much everything else."

"Exactly. You can give your mom information, but you can't make her respond a certain way. And when you *don't* try to control her, you're actually treating her with the utmost respect. You're creating a space where she is free to choose her behaviors."

"But what do I do now?"

Carrie shifted her chair so to face both Megan and her mom. "Hi, I'm Carrie." She smiled and reached out her hand.

The woman gave Carrie a trembling, weak handshake. "I'm Janey, Megan's mom."

"Thank you for being available to chat with us. Could you hear everything Megan told me? Is there anything you want us to repeat?"

The woman shook her head no.

"OK. I'm going to ask you a bit of a strange question. Tell me Janey, what do you really *really* want?"

She sat there, her eyes darting back and forth between Carrie and Megan. Carrie relaxed and gave her time to work the question through her mind.

Eventually, she answered in a quiet voice, "I want Megan to be normal."

"Tell me about that."

"To like boys, and to go to school every day, and to get a normal job so she doesn't have to rely on a man to pay for things."

"Alright. What do you want for you?"

"Me? I don't want anything! I just want Megan to be normal!"

"How important is it to have Megan in your life?"

"She's everything! I'd do anything for her!"

"So your relationship with her is more valuable than anything else in the world?"

"Definitely."

"That's a really powerful place to start. I know from talking to Megan previously, how much she values her relationship with you, too. What do you think about using the value of your relationship as a focus for everything we talk about?"

"What do you mean?"

"It means that no matter what you and Megan talk about, you'll make sure it's done with the utmost consideration for this relationship between the two of you." Carrie turned to Megan, "What do you think about that?"

"Yeah, I like that. It's easier to talk when I only have one thing to focus on. So I can focus on my mom's and my relationship." She turned to her mom, "I really love you. Like, a ton."

"I love you too, baby. But you can't like girls. You just can't."

"Hang on Janey. Remember that the most important thing is your relationship with Megan. If you try to control her or force her to behave a certain way, then you risk harming the relationship."

"But she'll never be happy if she's like that!"

"Is her happiness important to you?"

"Yes! Of course it is!"

"I think she'll be genuinely happy when she can be true to herself and have healthy, respectful relationships with you and with others. Would you be willing to listen to Megan as she works out what's important to her?"

"I... guess so?"

"It's OK to disagree with her. After all, you're still two different people, even though you're mother and daughter. But I think as you give her a safe space where she knows you love her and are there for her, you'll find a lot more in common. And if you don't, it's OK as long as you're both experiencing a healthy mother-daughter relationship."

Janey let out a sigh, "I want her to do what's right."

"OK, I'd like to suggest something. The word 'right' can be used to control what others do, and it sometimes creates barriers—which we don't want in relationships. What if we swapped out the word 'right' and instead we used words like 'effective' and 'responsible'? Are those things you'd like Megan to do?"

After a long pause, a single tear fell down Janey's cheek, "I hate the word 'right'. It's what my mom used all the time. She never listened to me, and always yelled at me for ignoring what was 'right'."

"Oh, Janey. That must have been so hard. I know your relationship with Megan can be different than that. Would you like to hear more about what your daughter's experiencing? When she's comfortable to share with you?"

She turned to Megan, and tentatively reached out and touched her cheek, "I want you to tell me everything. But right now, I'm kind of... full up?"

"Could we maybe talk with your help?" Megan asked Carrie, "Like, you could remind us if we're doing that controlling thing and stuff?"

"What do you think Janey? Could we take some time for this information to settle and meet together next week?"

"I can try…"

"Perfect! We'll make an appointment. Thank you so much for listening to Megan, and for prioritizing your relationship with her!" She paused, "Now there's just one more thing—it's seriously unsafe for Megan to be driving. I'd like you to give me your word that you will handle all the driving until Megan is legal to drive. It's essential to your safety, and to everyone else's." She turned to Megan, "Will you make the choice to not drive?"

"Um, mom? You OK with that?" Megan looked worried, and Carrie wondered how often she was expected to drive for her mom.

"OK, no more driving for Megan. I promise."

"Thank you!" Carrie stood up and walked to the door, "Alright you two, go out for ice cream, or do each other's nails, or watch a happy movie now, OK? Something that you can enjoy together."

"Maybe all three?" Megan asked, giving her mom a very compelling smile.

"I choose the nail color, you choose the movie."

"Deal!"

Carrie said goodbye to them and then closed the door and sat back down on her chair. The whole session had been challenging and emotional, and she needed some time to sort through her own thoughts. She blew out a long breath. If she had her laptop with her, she could type up a summary to send to her supervisor, which would also help her sort out her thoughts about the sudden counseling session. As it was, she'd have to do it as soon as she got home. There was just enough time before she needed to get Katie from school.

CHAPTER 2

"Hey Mom, I'm home!" Matthew dropped his backpack on the floor and kicked off his shoes before coming into the kitchen.

Carrie put down the knife she was cutting vegetables with and gave him a hug.

"What's that for?" he asked as he half-heartedly hugged her back.

"Just super glad you're you."

"Wait. You didn't have clients today. What happened?"

Carrie smiled. Matthew's ability to almost instantly perceive things going on with her was uncanny—but impressive. "I got called in for an emergency session with a mother and daughter. I think they'll be OK, but it just made me glad for what we have." She went back to her supper prep. "So, how was the club?"

Matthew had stayed after school to check out the LGBT club. Since becoming good friends with Liam, a transgender boy, he was developing an interest in how to help get equal treatment for everyone.

"It was OK, I guess. I mean, people were pretty suspicious of me being there because I'm straight and cis. But when Liam showed up and vouched for me it got better. It just makes me so frustrated that they expect everyone to mistreat them."

She mentally reviewed her growing vocabulary list: cis meant he identified with the gender he received at birth. "I expect them getting to know you, and vice versa, will help."

"I hope so." He opened the fridge and took out the leftover lasagna from the night before. "How long until supper?"

Carrie laughed, "Another hour, so you can eat a full meal now."

"Sweet!"

Matthew was still small for his age, but he had the appetite of a large man. Once Carrie realized that he really could eat a meal after school and still eat supper, she quit trying to control how big his 'snacks' were.

"Katie's at that thing?" he asked as he put a big plate of food into the microwave.

"Musical Theater club? Yep. Jonathan took her, so they should be back by supper. He said watching them is the best stress release!"

"He probably means he spends the whole time cracking up."

"Hey! That's entertainment too!"

The microwave dinged, and he took the plate into the living room and turned on the TV. Having Katie involved in more activities—and having Jonathan help with the driving—gave Matthew some much needed down time at home.

Carrie let her mind wander as she finished prepping veggies for a chicken stir-fry. It was hard to believe that only a few years ago she was a single mom struggling to recover from an abusive marriage, cope with an empty bank account, and support a son who was quiet and insecure.

Her first big break came from the dumpster—literally. A coffee table in decent condition caught her eye, and she brought it home, cleaned it up, and sold it for $40. She figured out how to upcycle furniture and picture frames and turned it into a business that now supported her and the kids completely.

In one of the rescued side tables she found $9,000 in cash, and with the encouragement of her friends she used it for tuition to complete her undergraduate degree in psychology, and then completed her master's in counseling psychology. When her practicum finished in two weeks' time, she would submit all the paperwork to become a licensed counseling psychologist.

Condensing it all into a few memories seemed too easy, but now the stress of paying bills, pinching pennies, and exchanging studying for sleep were behind. Plus, she was getting married to one of the world's nicest guys—something that she never imagined happening, but the thought of which now brought a huge smile to her face.

Neither of them were looking for love when they met. Jonathan's former fiancé had died in a car accident—along with the man she'd been having an affair with—and he had left the country to bury his anger and despair in his work. The only thing that convinced him to return was his sister-in-law Jenny's cancer diagnosis. He and Carrie met the day after he returned home, in a rather awkward coming-out-of-the-shower scene that would make an excellent story for years to come.

His small family—Jenny and his brother Max, their 7-year-old daughter Angela, and Jenny's parents—meant the world to him. Now he was adding Carrie, Matthew, Katie, and Carrie's parents to his family. Carrie knew how excited Jonathan felt about having the wife and children he had once dreamed of, and they both hoped to grow their family soon.

When Katie and Jonathan made it home, she was just finishing up the stir-fry. After an enthusiastic hug from Katie, and a knee-wobbling kiss from Jonathan, she sent them to wash up and called Matthew to set the table.

They ate most of their meals at Carrie's place, but after the wedding they'd all be moving to Jonathan's, just around the corner. He had been working hard to adapt the house to be wheelchair accessible for Carrie's mom, and her parents were staying there with the kids while Carrie and Jonathan went away for a short honeymoon. Then they would head off to Disneyland as a family!

Carrie watched Katie struggle to keep quiet at the table while everyone else talked about their day—a family rule Carrie tried to enforce—and then she let loose with a tsunami of words about everything from her theater class to details about playing with her friends at school, and her current favorite topic—Disneyland. It would be the kids' very first vacation beside trips to Carrie's parent's house an hour outside the city, and Katie could hardly contain her excitement.

After supper Carrie left Jonathan and Matthew to clean up while she helped Katie with her homework and reading. The quiet conversation and teasing coming from the kitchen was like listening to waves roll onto the shore at the lake—peaceful, soothing, and not to be taken for granted.

Her mind wandered back to a time when Matthew was starting second grade and desperate to show his daddy how well he could read. Don had the TV on and didn't want to be interrupted. Carrie almost always tried to referee situations like that, redirecting the kids until Don was more likely to give them some positive attention. But she was tired from a long night of Katie being sick with the flu, and her guard was down.

Don yelled, "Shut up Matthew! Can't you see I'm busy?" before turning back to the TV. Matthew had quietly gathered his home reading package, put it in his backpack, and gone into his room. He was a quick learner. He never tried to share anything with his dad again. At the time Carrie just hoped that her relationship with Matthew would be strong enough to make up for Don's multitude of sins.

But, in the past year Carrie watched as Matthew's relationship with Jonathan started to actually undo some of the damage Don had caused. Carrie figured they'd eventually come across things they disagreed about, but for now, Matthew was beginning to relax under the attention and respect that Jonathan gave him. He didn't call Jonathan 'Dad' yet, but when he was talking to Katie, he always referred to him as 'Daddy Jonny'—the nickname she gave him in the spring when Jonathan proposed to Carrie.

CHAPTER 3

Carrie drove to her practicum with a huge smile on her face. It was hard to believe that five and a half months ago, driving to the women's center was one of the scariest parts of her week. The women she met with were angry, frightened, and not afraid to say exactly what they thought of Carrie while Dr. Bradley, the psychologist on staff supervised her session while sitting in the corner of the room, offered up nothing but the odd unhelpful comment.

Maybe on the outside it didn't look like the women were changing, but Carrie knew better. Slowly they built trusting relationships. They knew about Carrie's struggles with her abusive ex and trying to start over. She knew about many of the situations and choices that led these women she now considered her friends to use the services at the center.

About a month into Carrie's sessions, she combined a craft project with a goal-setting mission. The women made cute little envelopes from the pages of old books. Then Carried asked them to write their answers to the question *What do you really, really want?* and put them in their envelopes.

None of them stuck with their first answers, which was part of the journey. As a group, they spent weeks talking with Carrie and each other about what they wanted, and slowly pulling away layers of lies and misinformation that had influenced what each of them thought and felt every day.

Sometimes inspiration arrived in a burst of tears, with the realization that she had been trying to please someone else her entire life. For others it was a slow process of writing down an answer, thinking about it, and then rewriting the answer.

Today each of them would read their revised answers and talk about how they were getting what they really really wanted, and Carrie could hardly wait to participate in the discussion.

She arrived just as Pamela, the receptionist, unlocked the door. A cigarette butt on the ground still gave off a waft of the smell that clung to her wherever she went. Carrie had decided early on not to do anything more than be polite to the surly woman, so she simply said, "Good morning" and waited for the door to open.

"I want to talk to you," Pamela started.

"Of course!" Carrie wondered what on earth she had done. The lady wasn't one for anything other than complaining. She followed her into the stale air of the reception area, and automatically turned on the old fan on the counter.

Pamela dropped her large purse on her chair and turned to face Carrie. "The girls have all been talking about that thing in the envelopes. So I did it too."

Carrie hoped her face looked interested, but inside she was going over her mental checklist to make sure she was ready for her group session.

"I want a different job."

That got Carrie's attention. "Tell me about that."

"When I was little something happened, and the power went off at our house. I was terrified of the dark back then and the thought of not having my light on at bedtime made me feel sick to my stomach. An electrician came and fixed it just before the sun went down. He became, like, my hero. Then my dad spent weeks complaining about how expensive it had been, and I decided I wanted to do the same thing—help people keep their lights on and make lots of money."

Carrie looked around the drab office where Pamela spent every day. It was in such contrast to what Pamela wanted, she felt terrible for what life must be like for her. "That's a bit of a change from where you are now."

"Well, thirty years ago a guidance counselor told me in no uncertain terms that I'd be a secretary, not an electrician. It's been bugging me ever since, but I just never thought about doing anything about it. Until now."

"So, where do you go from here?"

"I've been looking at college programs. I can get in and there's one that has evening classes."

There was something about the way she talked—full of hope, and certain she would fail at the same time.

"But I wish I had someone to help me study. You know, someone who knew stuff. I was never good at learning new things."

Carrie couldn't stop the smile that crossed her face, "Pamela! This is so incredible! There's a retired electrician who lives in an apartment near friends of mine. His name is Martin, and he's super nice. I was talking to him the other day, and he seemed discouraged because he doesn't have anything to do right now. What if you had a chat with him? I know he's taught my son and his friend some basic electrical things, and he can happily talk about his old work for forever."

Pamela was silent for a minute, before going to her purse and pulling out a cigarette. Carrie thought for a minute she'd light it, but she just rolled it through her fingers.

"You don't think it's a dumb idea?"

"Actually, I think it's a brilliant idea! In fact, I'll bet there are a lot of people out there that would prefer to hire a woman. And what a wonderful story about why you want to become an electrician!"

For the first time, Pamela smiled, "I'll need the number for your friend. And I'll put in a good word for you to replace Dr. Bradley. You belong here. He doesn't."

Just then the center's director walked in, followed by Dr. Bradley himself. Carrie and Pamela exchanged glances and burst out laughing at the same time.

"Celebrating the end of your practicum?" he asked.

"Oh no, quite the opposite!" Carrie managed to answer, before making eye contact with Pamela and laughing again.

At the end of the day, Carrie sat in the reception area at an empty desk beside Pamela's and wrote up her summary. It was true that she wanted to replace Dr. Bradley as the center's counselor once she was licensed, but she knew politics played a big part in the organization's hiring practices. Donna, the center's director, passed on an offer from the board for Carrie to continue on a volunteer basis. She had never met the board, but Pamela confided that they didn't like change so perhaps their offer (such as it was) was a compliment.

Donna seemed to hint that Dr. Bradley was well-established as the center's paid psychologist. Next week Carrie needed to decide what to do about the offer, and whether to give her contact information to the women she had worked with since the spring. There was no written rule that said she shouldn't, but she knew if she asked for permission she'd be told 'no'.

In the meantime, everyone in her group was making progress towards their goals. For some of them, things like not getting arrested again, or not being evicted, were the biggest challenges they could handle at the moment. But they were succeeding, and Carrie kept on encouraging them to add to their goals when they realized something else they wanted.

Many of them were starting to take responsibility for their own lives, and it had led to a few sharp, but effective one-liners that they continued to pass amongst themselves. They often used the infamous phrase 'How's that working for you?' when someone stuck to old habits but expected new results. When Carrie first used it, she was met with anger and resentment, but now the women were beginning to understand the intention and power behind the question.

Char was the first to confide in Carrie and through their work together Carrie began to have hope that she might make a difference at the center. Char was still with the boyfriend who used to beat her, but he had followed through with a suggestion to take an anger management class and the difference was noticeable.

The young couple met with Carrie every week during the summer, and they were working hard at building a healthy relationship. He was starting to respect Char and listen to her instead of controlling her, and Char was proud of the way he was changing his behaviors.

When Char was accepted into the Early Childhood Education program at the community college, he bragged about it to everyone they met. Carrie felt confident that in two years Char would be living her dream of being a preschool teacher.

Five and a half months ago, Carrie was counting the days until she completed her practicum at the center. Now she tried not to think about saying goodbye to all the women next week.

CHAPTER 4

"Wow, now that you're not watching the boys after school I feel like I never see you!"

"It's not like we ever had much time to talk during pick up and drop off, but I know what you mean." Carrie took a bite of her BLT and smiled across the table at Kara. A lot of where she was now was credit to her friend, but no matter how much she tried to thank her it was never enough.

Kara was the only one of Carrie's acquaintances who stood by her when she decided to leave her husband. Because he always acted sweet and charming in front of others, almost no one believed that life was so intolerable for Carrie. No one except Kara and Carrie's parents when she confided in them. When Kara hired Carrie to watch her three boys after school, it provided just enough income for Carrie to move out with Matthew and Katie.

Those next few years were tough, but Kara's belief in, and support of, her friend never faltered. Now, with Carrie working as an intern counseling psychologist one day a week at the clinic where Kara worked as a Physician's Assistant, they took advantage of the chance to have lunch together whenever their schedules allowed.

"Magnus seems to be doing better this year, at least from what I can see on the days I pick up Katie."

"He is. It's a credit to Ken really, for wanting to learn how to relate to him better. I mean, *you* always knew that Magnus had sensory challenges, but it wasn't until we got the autism spectrum diagnosis that we realized we needed to change some things in how we parent him."

She continued, after eating some fries, "And it's been really good for Justin and Calvin to learn that their little brother experiences the world differently. I think it's helped their fourteen-year-old brains to realize there's a world out there beyond rugby and video games."

Carrie reached over and rested her hand on Kara's arm. "You guys are doing awesome with your boys. Seriously."

Kara smiled back, "I guess we've all come a long way in the past few years. Who would've thought that Ken would become a stay-at-home dad, and you'd finish your schooling while building an epic business?"

"And don't forget Jaz's audacious housing project and the way she dragged us all into it!" Carrie added.

"I know. Oh to have the optimism of youth! I never dreamed it would work out so well. But I haven't talked to Lisa in a while. Are they still renting out the two suites on Airbnb?"

"Yeah. I guess we didn't plan on not having all the units occupied by regular tenants. But Lisa only opens bookings for a few weeks at a time, so as soon as a need comes up it'll be available. The accessible suite is always booked up. I mean, why stay in a poorly designed hotel room when you can stay in a proper accessible suite with a kitchen?"

Lisa had joined their group of friends courtesy of Kara's natural ability to connect people. They met at the clinic when Lisa brought her mom in to get help with her rheumatoid arthritis. Kara recognized the worn-out discouragement of a young caregiver and encouraged Lisa to call Carrie for support.

Growing up with a disabled parent, Carrie could relate to some of the challenges Lisa and Maria faced every day. They became friends, and then partners with Jaz in an ambitious plan to combine their resources and skillsets to create affordable housing. Now Lisa managed the six-unit building, and she and Maria were doing their best to adapt to Maria's health challenges.

Kara's voice interrupted Carrie's reminiscing about her friends. "Speaking of accessible, how are the renovations to Jonathan's house going?"

"Well, I'm so sad he had to gut that gorgeous bathroom to make it accessible for Mom. But he donated the original fixtures to the Habitat for Humanity Re-store, so at least it wasn't wasted. Oh, and I got a whole load of frames for me and prints for Lauren when we dropped off our donations. I never even thought of checking them out before. So that was a sweet find."

"I'm so happy your parents will finally get to visit you at your home —well, soon to be your home. That's been a long time coming!"

"The kids are so excited to have them around. With them not being able to visit here before, they've missed out on all the usual grandparent things—seeing the kids' school, and where they go for activities and stuff."

"You busted your ass for so long and made so many sacrifices with hardly anything to show for it. You deserve everything good that comes your way now. I hope you can accept that."

Carrie gazed at Kara for a minute before answering. She wondered if it was obvious that she struggled to believe she could have a good life. "Thanks. I'm working on it. And I guess now we have to get ourselves back to work!"

They quickly made their way back to the clinic, suddenly conscious of time and long lists of patients and clients.

Carrie's last session of the day was with Megan and her mom Janey.

"So, did you two do anything different this past week in your relationship?"

With a proud smile, Janey started, "I didn't let Megan drive once!"

Carrie smiled, "Excellent! That's a pretty important boundary. What happened when you weren't feeling up to driving?"

"Sometimes we just didn't go. And once I made myself drive anyways to take Megan for a job interview at a grocery store. I think she's going to get it, too!"

Carrie felt her heart sink. In her mind, Megan had enough to handle. She was battling anxiety, not always making it to school, and figuring out her sexuality. A job could put more strain on her. *But it's not about what I think* she reminded herself.

"OK Megan. How did the week go for you?"

"Um, good at home. I just... knowing Mom is trying to accept me no matter what is a pretty big deal. I was reading online about people coming out and stuff and there's lots of scary stories about parents freaking out. That's why I didn't plan on saying anything. But I'm glad I did now."

"And school?"

Her gaze dropped, and she started pulling at the skin around her nails. "It's a lot of work. You know, to pretend I'm like everyone else. I'm lucky these girls let me hang around with them. But if they ever knew..."

Carrie knew statistics were against Megan. Gay and lesbian high-schoolers were many times more likely to commit suicide because of the hostile environments they faced—not because of their identity. Having a supportive family improved the odds, but they still faced a tide of discrimination, rejection, and worse at a time when life-changes were overwhelming.

"It's always your choice what you tell people, and who you tell. This is *your* story Megan. No one else's. Janey, that's a good little tidbit for you, too. When it comes to talking to extended family, this is Megan's story to tell as she chooses. That might be hard to get used to."

The mother and daughter exchanged glances, "We already talked about that. At least we don't see my family very often — I think they wouldn't be nice about it."

"You guys have a lot of challenges to deal with. And there are other families out there in similar situations. I want to emphasize that this is nobody's fault. Yes, this is a challenging road. And I know some things won't get easier. I'm sorry about that. But I'm also so proud of the way you're both working on communicating and respecting each other. I wish more people would follow your lead!"

"The things you said last week got stuck in my head. Like how telling her to do what's right is me trying to control her. I thought I was a pretty laid back mom. You know, like letting her do her own thing, and not making her go to school. But there's other ways I'm kinda controlling."

"It's a mom thing, isn't it? I do the same thing with my kids. But when we see ourselves doing it, we can stop and change our approach. That's the beauty of relationships! We're always working to have healthier connections with each other. And even when Megan makes mistakes, it's OK. We do a lot of learning that way!"

"I wish people could learn about this. The girls at school, it's like all they do is try and make you be like them. Everything's about control."

"Have you thought about getting to know some other people? Girls and boys?"

"Sort of. I just — these girls already think I'm normal. New friends might see through that."

"Well, normal's just something everyone pretends to be. Try to remember that. I'm guessing most of the girls are all trying to be something they think others will like. The good news is, we do start to find ourselves, and many people become more authentic over time. But normal? I wouldn't try too hard for that!"

"I always felt like I was trying to fit in back then," Janey admitted.

"See? It's something that happens to a lot of us. But keep your eyes out for people who might be more comfortable as themselves. It might just mean smiling and saying hi to others once in a while. And it's so great that you can come home and relax with your mom."

"Yeah. That actually makes going to school a little easier. You know, that it's only part of the day."

Carrie stopped herself from saying a job could be stressful too. Despite all her training so far, there were times when she really wanted to 'fix' things. But that wasn't her job. She changed the topic to a more general discussion about relationships. Both Janey and Megan actively participated, and they ended the session with everyone feeling positive and having new, healthy strategies for relating to each other. *That* was her job.

CHAPTER 5

"Annie Cawie!"

"Hi Brittany! Come on in!" Carrie called from the basement. She grabbed the basket of folded laundry and hurried upstairs. Setting it down, she reached for Brittany and gave her a big hug. "Aunty Carrie missed you!"

"Me too Annie Cawie!"

Putting the little girl down, Carrie turned to her mom Lauren, her arms stretched around a batch of finished paintings. They met when Lauren was pregnant with Brittany, and neither realized how their friendship would change both of their lives.

At first, Lauren worked with Carrie upcycling frames for Carrie's business. But Lauren's art background made her a visionary. When she saw all the bland artwork people left at thrift stores, she started a side-business transforming each painting into a new work of art.

Lauren's paintings sold on Carrie's website and contributed significantly to the bottom line. It also paid for the care her husband Dustin needed, as he dealt with brain damage from a tragic drug overdose. It was a unique partnership between the two women, but it worked.

"It looks like you got past your painter's block!" Carrie crouched down to look at one of the finished products. Lauren always sent a 'before' picture, and it was the only way to truly appreciate the transformation she could create. Recently Lauren had struggled to come up with ideas, and she spent almost a week agonizing about her possible lost revenue.

But the painting in front of her proved she had her groove back. Lauren usually worked with landscapes, adding in wildlife, cottages, or people that gave the paintings life and depth. This one started out as a typical abstract piece with triangles and blocks of color on a white background, and Lauren added tiny handwritten words and phrases along the sharp edges of the blocks of color.

Face the sun, keep the shadows behind you.

Love with open hands.

You matter, more than you can imagine.

When a door closes, try the handle.

A little step everyday will make dreams come closer.

"Lauren! This is amazing! And it looks so elegant, too. Where did you get the idea?"

"Well, I got super ticked-off and stormed out of the house because I couldn't figure out what to do, and Dustin kept trying to talk to me instead of using his word pad. I ended up at that fancy art gallery downtown and started looking at the people looking at the paintings. They're all acting like they're super smart, you know, looking closely at the paintings and stuff. And I was like, there's nothing there to see, idiots! And then 'boom!' I was like, 'I'll give them something to see'. So I came home and did this!"

"I love it! Any ideas what to call it?" Carrie and Lauren named and priced each print together before Carrie took over the listing and sale.

"What about 'Background Vibes' or something?"

"Maybe just 'Background Vibe'?

"Yep!" She put her hand in the air, and Carrie high-fived her.

Together they looked through the other four paintings, choosing prices and names. If everything sold, Lauren would take home $800, and Carrie would keep $80. Not bad for a week's worth of work for Lauren, and about an hour for Carrie.

"Can you even believe we're still doing this?" Carrie asked as she headed to the kitchen to make coffee. Brittany chattered happily to herself while playing with the basket of toys in the living room, and Lauren was stacking the prints by the back door for Carrie to photograph before listing them.

"I know. Crazy!" Lauren slouched in a chair at the table and propped her feet up in another chair. People often struggled to match the rough-looking woman with the artist and classical music lover, but to Carrie it made perfect sense. Lauren was all about heart and soul, and her own image had nothing to do with her talents.

"So, this is kind of last minute, but I wondered if you had time to do a session with the women at the center next Monday morning?"

"A session? What the heck does that mean?"

"Well, I thought you could bring a picture, and just do your magic right there in front of them while you talk about how things can look different when you take the time to add your own color to life."

Lauren nearly snorted out the sip of coffee she had just taken. "You never stop with the fluffy happy stuff, do you?"

"Hey! This is real! You create amazing art every single day from the stuff other people throw out! There's a pretty powerful lesson there!

I just wish I would have thought of it sooner, since next week is my last week."

"You're not going back?"

"I don't think so. I've been going back and forth about it for a while, but Dr. Bradley is on some sort of contract and he refuses to cancel it. I suspect there are some connections with the board behind the scenes. I'm not interested in working there if he's still around."

"Even though they deserve better than an asshole like him?"

"I agree with you. I'm just not up for being the volunteer who does all the work while he takes the credit if anyone does well, and the paycheck every month. I'm going to leave my contact information with all the women, and they know they can touch base whenever. It just won't happen under the women's center umbrella for now."

"OK. So I'll show up Monday and be your success story."

"Hey, you made your own success story. I just profit off it!" Carrie smiled. Spending time with Lauren helped her stay grounded. She always challenged Carrie to be authentic and not get too carried away with the success of her business.

The oven timer interrupted them. "You *still* use that stupid timer?"

"You wait 'til you have to remember to pick Brittany up from school and then we'll talk. Did you want to hang out here until the kids get home? We can do second cups of coffee."

"Naw, I'll leave now. Brittany will freak out if I try to leave while they're here."

Carrie grabbed their empty mugs and moved them to the sink. "OK. So I'll see you Monday at nine at the women's center?"

"Nine! What the heck do you think I am, the morning sunshine?" Lauren tried to glare at Carrie, but her face broke into a smile too quickly to be taken seriously. "Yeah, yeah. Nine." She got up and hugged Carrie before going to grab her daughter. "Love ya babe!"

31

"Love you too Lauren! And you Brittany!"

Brittany reluctantly put the toys down and stood up, "Bye Annie Cawie!"

Brittany's sweet voice echoed in Carrie's ear as she walked to the school to get Katie. No matter how rough the little family's start had been, with going from living in a shelter, to struggling to cope after Dustin's overdose and permanent disabilities, Brittany was proof that children made everything better.

She wondered how long it would be before her family would hear more little voices in their home. They both wanted to have more children and were hoping that it wouldn't be long before Carrie was expecting.

While waiting for the bell to ring, she felt her phone vibrating in her back pocket. Seeing her dad's number pop up, she quickly answered. "Hi Dad!"

"Hi Care Bear." His voice sounded strained and weak and Carrie's heart began pounding as she considered a rash of terrible scenarios.

"What's wrong?"

"Well, we were really hoping things would get better with your wedding so close, but your mom's not doing so well." He exhaled shakily.

She tried to ignore the sinking feeling in her stomach. When it wasn't physical problems and chronic pain, her mom struggled with occasional bouts of depression. The timing couldn't be worse with the wedding so close. "What's going on?"

"Well, she got a cold a few weeks ago. You know how it is when she gets a cough…"

Carrie's mom had been permanently disabled in a car accident when Carrie was ten years old. Carrie became a caregiver for her mom and little sister overnight, while her dad worked long hours to provide for his family, and she knew from experience that a lingering cough could become something much worse due to limited movement.

"Did you take her in?" she asked, although she already knew the answer. Her mom avoided doctors and hospitals no matter how bad she felt, and it was always a battle when she needed specialized care. If her dad was calling, it was probably because he needed help convincing her to go to the doctor.

"Yeah. Last night she just couldn't catch her breath. I was afraid it would be too much for her to get to the car so I called an ambulance. I'm sorry I took so long to call you, but we were waiting to see the specialist. It's pneumonia, Carrie. I'm so sorry I didn't catch it sooner."

It felt like her world started spinning out of control around her while simultaneously grinding to a halt. This could change everything. Her mom hadn't spent a night in the hospital since she left after the accident. No matter what, she always managed to stay at home.

She heard a long sniff from the other end of the phone.

"Dad, this is *not* your fault, OK? And I'm so glad you called for an ambulance last night. You did the right thing." Carrie was interrupted by the bell ringing. "Listen, I'm picking Katie up from school and it's about to get really loud here. Can I call you back in ten minutes when I get home?"

"Yes, of course. Give Katie my love and I'll talk to you in a few minutes."

"Bye Dad. I love you." Carrie put the phone back in her pocket with a shaking hand. She swallowed hard a few times and looked up at the sky, blinking quickly. Pneumonia was serious. And scary. It must've been really bad for her dad to call an ambulance. She needed to figure out how to get there as soon as possible.

Absentmindedly she greeted Katie and smiled at a few parents and kids before turning towards home. She needed a plan in place before telling the kids—and having to deal with Katie's emotions and questions.

Katie chatted away on the walk home, blissfully unaware of the crisis facing her family. Matthew arrived home at the same time, and Carrie told them to grab a snack and watch TV while she made an important call.

In her room, she crawled onto her bed and hugged a pillow to her stomach while she called her dad back.

"Hi Dad. So what do you know right now?" She wished he could tell her that everything would be fine and her mom was on her way home with antibiotics that could fix everything.

"They have her on IV antibiotics, and steroids to reduce inflammation, and oxygen of course. Her levels are a bit better now, but she's still so distressed Carrie." His voice broke and Carrie ached for him.

"OK. I'll be there as soon as I can. Go stay with Mom. I'll text you when I'm on my way."

"Thank you," he whispered.

Carrie hung up and called Jonathan. She knew he was working hard so he could take time off next week, but everything had suddenly changed. "Hey. I just got off the phone with Dad. Mom's in the hospital with pneumonia and it's bad. I need you to stay with the kids so I can get there as soon as possible."

"I'll be right over," he answered and hung up.

Minutes later he stood in her room holding her while she cried. "Don't worry about anything here, OK? The kids and I will be fine. You focus on your mom."

Together they went downstairs to tell the kids what was happening, and then she quickly packed and said goodbye to her little family. Her heart ached as she left them and turned her car towards her hometown.

CHAPTER 6

Carrie tried to concentrate on driving and not let her mind wander, but it was impossible. She kept picturing her mom, helpless in a hospital bed, struggling for every breath. As kids, she and her little sister Jessica were always careful to wash their hands lots and stay away from sick kids, but every year her mom would get a cold that would leave her bed-ridden for weeks. During those times Carrie took over managing everything in the house while her dad continued to work long hours as a mechanic so he could cover the additional medical expenses.

The never-ending effects of that car accident were the reason Jessica became a personal injury lawyer and Carrie knew she was relentless in the courtroom. People thought that getting a big payout fixed everything. Someone even called her mom 'lucky' for getting a settlement. But the money only paid for them to buy a single story house, and hadn't covered the costs of adapting the house or van for a wheelchair, or any other thing their family had to do or change to make her mom comfortable in the years to follow. And now again her mom was paying the price for something that happened decades earlier.

When she got to the small community hospital she hurried down to the ward she knew her mom would be on. The familiarity of the hospital helped her navigate but didn't ease the pain of seeing her mom looking so pale and small in the hospital bed. Her eyes were closed, so Carrie quietly went around to her dad and hugged him.

He was sitting on a vinyl covered chair, his graying hair a little messy, his eyes red and tired-looking, wearing a button-up shirt and khakis that had clearly been slept in.

"You alright?" she whispered.

"Better with you here."

Her mom's eyes fluttered open, and she looked confused for a minute before settling her gaze on Carrie.

"Hi Mom," she said while gently reaching to hug her. "You're not looking so great, you know?"

She opened her mouth to say something but began coughing. Carrie quickly reached around to support her back and shoulders. The shudder of every cough was agonizing. Finally her coughing slowed down, and Carrie laid her back down and reached for the cup of water with a straw in it. Her mom only took a sip before laying back down and closing her eyes.

The next few hours were spent trying to keep her comfortable while they waited for the doctor to finish with his clinic visits and return to the hospital for rounds. For the first time, Carrie seriously considered the benefits of moving her parents to the city. At least they'd have immediate access to specialists when they needed them. Her mind buzzed with possibilities and worries, as she helplessly listened to her mom's labored breathing and watched her dad clench his jaw and rub his face.

By the time the doctor made it to the room, they were tense and exhausted.

"Hello, Julia! Always nice to see you, although I'd prefer difference circumstances." He walked over for a closer look at the machine monitoring her vital signs. "Not up to conversations yet though, are you?"

She shook her head 'no' but pointed to Carrie.

"Carrie! Hello!"

"Hi Dr. Morgan. When can Mom come home?"

He looked down at a clipboard in his hand before meeting Carrie's gaze. "I've asked for a second opinion on her chest x-rays. They don't look good." He turned back to his patient. "I know you don't need a lecture, but you really need to get on antibiotics as soon as you start to feel something coming on. Once that infection takes hold, it's really hard to get rid of it."

"I think we were hoping it would clear up on its own," her dad said apologetically. "I'm sorry. You're right." He turned to Carrie. "I'm so sorry this is happening now. We wanted to be there for *you* not the other way around."

"Dad, stop. Let's just focus on Mom getting better. Everything else doesn't matter right now, OK?"

The doctor cleared his throat, and they both turned back to him. "If Julia gets any worse, I want her transferred to Saint Mary's in the city." He held up his hand to stop Julia who was shaking her head 'no'. "I know you don't want to go there. But we simply can't provide the level of care here that they can. We'll do our best, but I will not compromise your chances of getting better if it comes to it. And in the meantime, you know we're all aiming for the very best outcome."

He turned to Carrie and her dad. "I'd ask you two to go home and get some rest, but I know you won't listen. One of the nurses will bring in a cot, and there's an empty bed next door, too. John, I need you to leave Julia to Carrie and the nurses tonight and you take the room next door. We've got room at the inn tonight, so we might as well use it."

For the moment, Carrie was grateful the hospital was willing to bend the rules. She'd insist on sleeping in her mom's room so her dad could get a proper sleep. It looked like he hadn't gotten much rest in the last few days.

"Dad, I'm going to head out to get some supper for us, and then you're going to go sleep in the other room for the night."

He sank back into his chair. "OK, dear. Thank you."

She kissed her mom's cheek and stepped outside the room. A minute later the doctor joined her and they walked down the hallway together.

"I'm glad you're here. I've never seen her as bad as last night. It was a close one."

Carrie blew out a breath. "What do I need to know?"

"Wait until all the test results come back. If her lungs can recover, she'll be OK. But I'm worried the damage may be permanent."

"Well, if she needs to move to Saint Mary's, let's do that sooner rather than later, OK?"

He nodded. "Go get your dad some decent supper. I'll stick around until you're back. The nurses know you're here. We'll do everything we can."

"Thanks Dr. Morgan."

As soon as she stepped outside, she took deep breaths of the clean air and tried to release some of the stress and worry. But when she got to her car, the tears started to fall and she couldn't stop them. Unable to drive, she gave in to the need to cry. She desperately wished Jonathan could be here with her, while being grateful he took over with the kids so she could come right away.

When she was finally calm enough to drive, she headed to the small downtown area where she ordered matzo ball soup and Rueben sandwiches from a little deli. Wanting to avoid having to make small talk, she went back to the car to wait for the order to be ready and called Jonathan.

The kids wanted to talk first, and she assured them that Grandma was being taken care of in the hospital, and she'd send their love along. She didn't know how much to tell them, so she kept most of the conversation focused on their day.

Matthew had spent the evening at a friends' playing guitar and just gotten back home. Carrie was grateful he had some good friends whose parents didn't mind driving their kids to each other's houses.

Katie was her usual chatty self, talking about everything she did at gymnastics, the funny joke her teacher told at school, and how Daddy Johnny was being silly with her home reading.

"How are you?" Jonathan asked when the kids were done talking.

Tears welled up in her eyes again. "This one's really bad. The doctor's worried that her lungs are so damaged they won't recover. And there's a chance they'll have to move her to the city for better care."

"Geez Carrie, that's rough! How's your dad?"

"He looks terrible. I'm just picking up some supper, and then I'll sleep in Mom's room tonight and he'll sleep in one of the empty hospital beds next door. It's probably been at least a week that he's been up at night with her, judging by how sick she is."

There was a pause on the other end before he continued, "I wish I could make this all better for you. At least everything's covered on this end. You just focus on your parents. And if... if at any time you feel I should bring down the kids, just say the word. We can be there in just over an hour."

Carrie tried to take a deep breath, but her chest felt all tight and her ribs refused to move. She hated to consider the possibility of things getting worse. "Thanks. I love you."

"Love you too."

A tap on her window startled her, and she rolled it down. The restaurant owner passed her a takeout bag. "That should be everything you need. Tell your mom we're praying for her."

Carrie thanked him and drove away. There were definitely some nice things about small towns.

CHAPTER 7

The night dragged on for Carrie. Whenever she started to doze off, her mom's coughing woke her up. It seemed like the nurses were constantly in and out, adjusting her mom's position, replacing IV bags, and at one point calling the doctor to discuss a hospital transfer. Carrie found herself watching the oxygen saturation number on the monitor, willing it to stay above 93% so her mom wouldn't be moved.

The bustle of nurses doing their morning care routine woke Carrie up, although she didn't feel like she had slept at all. She struggled to open her eyes until she realized a nurse was trying to work around the cot. Quickly she got up and pushed it further away from the hospital bed.

"Sorry for waking you hon," another nurse said. "But maybe you'd like to grab a coffee while we get your mom changed?"

"Yeah, of course," she mumbled. Leaning over she kissed her mom's cheek, grateful to see she wasn't any worse. She grabbed the overnight bag she had quickly packed and slipped into the bathroom to change and freshen up. Although she knew it was clean and sanitized, she still fought against the idea that she shouldn't touch anything. There was always something about hospital bathrooms that made her not want to use them.

Peeking in to see her dad still sleeping, she made her way to the cafeteria. The hospital smells got stronger as she passed by the long-term care ward. The idea that one day her mom might have to live in a place like that was an intrusion she didn't need this morning.

With wistful thoughts of the good coffee waiting for her at home, she added enough cream and sugar to the hospital coffee to make it palatable. Thinking the nurses would need some more time, she sat down at a window overlooking the hospital grounds and took out her phone.

Already there were loving messages from all of her friends and promises to help out with the kids and anything else needed. But it was Maria's message that stopped Carrie short.

We're all thinking about you and sending love and prayers. Whatever you need for the wedding, we can make it happen.

It was Friday morning. That meant her wedding was supposed to be one week from tomorrow. And Maria was right. They needed a new plan. On the off chance that Jonathan and the kids were still sleeping, she decided to wait and call him after she knew the kids were at school. Instead, she texted a short good morning message to him.

Looking around the cafeteria she was grateful to see it nearly empty. Conversation with strangers—or even acquaintances, since almost everyone in town knew her family—wasn't what she wanted this morning.

Sipping her coffee, she tried to think of how to make things work but her brain just wouldn't cooperate. Images of her mom looking so frail took over all other thoughts. She resisted the temptation to lay her head on the table, afraid that she might fall asleep. Finally, she figured she had given them enough time. Getting another coffee for her dad, she made her way back to the ward.

The nurse was just bundling the dirty sheets into a cart outside the room. "Your mom's looking better this morning!" she said cheerfully.

"She is?"

"Definitely. Oxygen levels are good, and her lungs are sounding a bit better."

Carrie felt tears of gratitude fill her eyes. "Thank you," she whispered.

"You go in there and see your mom. I'm going to bring her a cup of tea and toast, and then she'll need to rest again."

Nodding her head, Carrie walked in. She couldn't see what the nurse saw. Her mom's face was pale, and her light-brown shoulder-length hair looked limp. The clean hospital gown had already slipped off one side, showing more pale skin and a bony protrusion for her shoulder. Her neck muscles still pulled a bit with every breath, and Carrie wondered where she found the energy to keep trying.

Her eyes fluttered open. "Hi, Care Bear," she whispered with a weak smile.

"Mom," she croaked, unable to stop the tears from flowing. "You're looking a little better!" She reached over and kissed her cheek.

"You look beautiful!" her mom answered softly.

"I'm just so relieved you're OK. That was a close one, you know?" She held up her hand to stop any unnecessary effort. "Don't worry about talking. I know you were just hoping you'd get better on your own. The nurse is coming with tea and toast in a few minutes. Do you need a drink?"

She nodded, and Carrie brought the cup and straw over. Seeing her mom have energy for more than just a sip gave her hope. She set the cup down, lowered the side rail of the hospital bed and carefully readjusted her mom's gown so she could wiggle onto the bed and rest her head on her mom's shoulder.

It brought back a flood of memories of being a little girl, trying to have some contact with her mom after the accident, but terrified that the smallest movement might hurt her. They figured it out, with little Carrie lying beside her, holding her mom's hand gently while resting her head on her shoulder. She often stayed like that beside her mom until she could feel her relax as the pain medication kicked in. It was still a familiar place for her to be, but always bittersweet as she wished for an easier life for her mom.

A few minutes later Carrie's dad came in, looking a little better himself. He had smoothed out his hair and carefully tucked his wrinkled shirt into his pants. Carrie pointed to the coffee she brought for him and he smiled gratefully before walking around and kissing his wife.

"Good morning love. It's good to have our girl here, isn't it?"

Carrie felt her nod, and her dad pulled the chair as close as possible while he drank his coffee. When the orderly came in with breakfast, Carrie helped her mom eat and was relieved to see she ate almost a full piece of toast. She knew it couldn't possibly be enough to fuel a recovery, but it was a start.

After her mom fell asleep again, Carrie quietly slipped out with her dad close behind. She hugged him and then stepped back.

"Did you sleep last night?"

"I did. Thanks for being here."

"Anytime Dad. The nurse said she's a little better this morning. Maybe we'll get away with keeping her here and not moving her to another hospital."

"I hope so. Are you feeling up to driving me home? I need a change of clothes, and I think your mom would like a few of her things."

"Of course! Let's just stick around until the doctor comes through, OK?"

"Right. Forgot about that. Let's go get some breakfast from the cafeteria then. Hospital toast is just about as good as at home, isn't it?"

"Just about," Carrie agreed. She stopped at the nurses' station to make sure they'd page her if the doctor came by. The casual atmosphere of the small hospital made it easy to step out for a few minutes, knowing someone would call them.

After eating, they ended up sharing the elevator with the doctor, and together the three of them walked to the hospital room. He agreed that things were looking better but warned that she would need to stay in the hospital until they were certain the infection was gone, and she could transfer on and off the toilet without too much strain.

"We can't risk getting her body too run down. Let's take the time to get it cleared up properly. I hope we'll continue to make positive progress from here."

Driving home, Carrie's dad brought up the one thing they had all been thinking. "I'm afraid we won't be up for making it to your wedding or watching the kids after. I'm so sorry Carrie."

"Dad, that doesn't matter. We'll figure something else out. Just take care of mom, and take care of yourself, too. OK?"

He nodded and looked out the side window as Carrie drove.

After showers, fresh clothes, and packing a case of her mom's favorite things, they were on their way back to the hospital. Seeing her mom still asleep Carrie went back outside to call Jonathan. The clock read 8:57, but she felt she had been up for an entire day.

"Hey there. How are things?"

His voice made Carrie start crying all over again. "I'm OK, honest!" she said, smiling through her tears. "It's just so good to hear your voice. Mom had a really rough night, but she's a bit better this morning. Dad got some sleep, although he's still quite tired. How are things there?"

"Fine. Katie said extra prayers for all of you at every meal and at bedtime, and Matthew wanted you to know he loves you and everything's fine here."

"That's good. Thanks so much for being there!"

"Of course. So what's next for your mom?"

"She's definitely going to stay in the hospital until she's completely better. I'm guessing at least until next week sometime..." she paused, not wanting to disappoint him. He had been determined that Carrie would have everything she wanted for a wedding.

"I guess we get to make new plans then, huh?"

"What are you thinking?" Carrie desperately hoped he wouldn't suggest delaying it, and then felt guilty for being so selfish.

"Didn't you say you grew up going to the church there with your family?"

"Yeah..."

"Well, what if we take the wedding to your mom? Either we can use the church there, or if she's still in the hospital, we'll just take over the cafeteria for a little ceremony!"

"Oh Jonathan, do you really mean it? I know you've been so excited about our plans. I hate to disappoint—"

"—Carrie," he interrupted firmly, "the only thing that matters is who I'm marrying. Where, or how—that doesn't matter."

"But what about the reception?"

"I don't know. I'll give the restaurant a call when they open at 11:30 and see what we can work out. And are you OK sending a text to your friends to see if anyone might be able to take Matthew and Katie? If not, we can delay our honeymoon until later."

"Uh, yeah. OK. Gosh, I hadn't really thought about that. I was just trying to steel myself to postpone everything. But if you think it's OK…"

"We can delay Disneyland too if we need to. I don't want to be far away if your mom's not better."

"Thank you," she whispered, fighting the tears that threatened to start falling again. How did she get such a good, kind, considerate fiancé? "I'm so lucky to have you!"

"You're my life, Carrie. We'll get through this, OK? And try not to worry about anything. You're where you need to be right now, and the kids and I are fine. That's all that matters."

"Thanks again. I'll send out a text, but we'll just have to play everything by ear. And I'm sure the pastor will be by to visit mom today, so I'll ask him if the church is free next Saturday." She smiled, "It's a cute church."

"Let me call the church here and let them know our plans have changed. Do you want me to see if this pastor can make it down to do the ceremony still?"

"Only if the Pastor Leung from here can't do it. I'll text you when I know. And I guess everyone can just drive down here for the ceremony?"

"Of course. Maybe we'll set up a caravan or something. It'll be fun!"

"Aw, that sounds neat! OK, I'm feeling a bit better about the wedding stuff. Especially now that I know we don't have to postpone it." She let out a sound that was a half laugh, half cry. "Oh my goodness. I don't know what I'm feeling about everything. Happy. Sad. Worried. Hopeful."

"Hey, this has been a brutal week for you. I think most women just get overwhelmed with their wedding and you've got us, and your practicum, and your mom's health crisis to deal with too. You've got this Carrie, and I've got you so we'll be OK."

She felt her throat start to constrict, "How did I get so lucky with you?"

He laughed, "As long as you always feel you're lucky to be with me! I love you, Carrie. More than anything else."

"I love you too. But I guess I'd better get back inside and check on Mom."

CHAPTER 8

The rest of Friday and Saturday Carrie and her dad traded off sitting in the hospital room and trying to pass the time. With nothing tangible to do it became a rotating wait-and-see routine. Wait and see how long until the next coughing fit. Wait and see what the next vitals check showed. Wait and see whether the doctor felt things were going OK, or whether a hospital transfer was in order. Wait and see if her mom ate, or drank, or slept.

Pastor Leung's visit was a welcome change. Although Carrie's mom still couldn't say more than a few words without coughing, they sat around the bed and talked about the wedding, with her nodding and smiling her agreement. They planned a simple, traditional ceremony followed by a little reception in the church hall.

On Sunday morning Carrie and her dad stepped away from the hospital to go to church together. It was a relief to get a break from the hospital, even though they both were reluctant to leave.

When they walked into the church, she instantly felt enveloped by love and support. These were the same people that had stood by her family after the car accident, and they all knew and loved Carrie and the entire family.

The pastor announced that the church would celebrate her wedding to Jonathan on Saturday and then shocked Carrie by asking if people could contribute to a buffet after the ceremony. He suggested the idea to Carrie when they talked at the hospital, but she didn't think many people would be interested in helping. She was wrong. Nearly everyone raised their hands, and she gave teary smiles of gratitude to the people around her.

Suddenly, their wedding ceremony was transforming into a celebration with old family friends contributing to a reception in true small-town style. It was better than she could have wished for, with a lot more people coming to the ceremony and she was thrilled to be surrounded by so many wonderful people. What a perfect way to get married!

That afternoon she got more good news. Lisa was happy to come over and stay with the kids in lieu of her parent's watching them so that Carrie and Jonathan could still go on their honeymoon.

She FaceTimed the kids and Jonathan with the new plan. Katie's eyes got wide with excitement. "You mean Lisa will be here for three whole days? Do you think Jaz and Alex and Maria could visit? We could have pizza!" She turned behind her, "Daddy Johnny, can you buy pizza for Lisa so we can have a party when you're gone with Mommy?"

He called back that he could, and Katie jumped up and down with excitement. Matthew's response was quieter, and he promised Carrie that he'd help Lisa with everything.

Carrie's mom now had enough breath to apologize profusely for getting sick and ruining everyone's plans, but Carrie refused to entertain such things. Instead, she positioned herself on the bed and carefully rested her head on her mom's shoulder.

"You can't help the fact that you got sick Mom. It is what it is. And spending your days feeling guilty won't help you get better. So just stop it!" She said her words with a smile, but she meant it. It was a relief just to see her mom have the energy to talk a little bit, and her coughs were not as all-consuming as they had been a few days earlier.

"Alright Care Bear. I'll try. And when I'm better, we'll come stay at your lovely new house so you and Jonathan can get away."

"Thanks, Mom. I can't even believe that in a week I'll be married."

"He seems like a good man."

"He is Mom. He is. And he's been so wonderful with Matthew and Katie too. We're all so lucky!"

"And you *will* go back this evening so you can finish off your practicum, right?"

There had been some heated discussions between Carrie and her parents about the upcoming week. She insisted she should stay with them until her mom was home from the hospital, but they wouldn't hear of it.

It was her younger sister Jessica who settled the matter. Originally, she planned to spend the week before the wedding with Carrie. Instead, she offered to drive straight to the hospital when her flight arrived on Monday. That only left Sunday night with their parents on their own, and they insisted they'd be fine.

Like only a sister could, Jessica bluntly told Carrie to get over herself the next time she called to check on everyone. "Carrie, you've got to stop acting like you're the only one who can do any good for Mom and Dad. Seriously, I've got this. I'll be there on Monday after-noon. It's stupid for you to delay your practicum completion when nobody's dying."

"You're right Jess. I guess. But you have to promise me that if you think Mom's taking a turn for the worse, you'll call me right away."

"Not happening. Mom will keep getting better, and I'll make sure she and Dad are ready for your big day."

"Fine." Carrie sighed and slumped back in her chair. She couldn't be bothered to argue—especially when she knew deep down that her sister was right. "But I'm sad we won't get the time to hang out together this week."

"Me too. Guess we'll put it on the wish list, huh? I love you sis, but I'd better get back to work here. See you Wednesday night!"

Carrie promised to drive straight back to the hospital on Wednesday evening after her shift at the clinic. It would give her a little time with her sister. Thank goodness Jonathan could take care of everything with the kids.

Driving home Sunday night with nothing else to occupy her mind, Carrie found herself counting the minutes down. She really missed the kids and Jonathan at night, when the sounds of the hospital kept her awake in spite of her exhaustion. Now those feelings were nearly overwhelming, and she desperately needed to hug the people she loved. Thank goodness her family had insisted she go home for a few days!

She hadn't even turned the car off before Katie was tearing out of the house screaming, "Mommy! Mommy!" with Matthew close behind.

Carrie kneeled on the cool grass in the front yard and felt the therapeutic effects of her children's unconditional love work their way into her soul.

"I really really missed you!" Katie said into Carrie's shoulder.

"I missed you too! All of you!" She looked up to see Jonathan standing close by, waiting for the kids to get their fill of their mom.

"How's Grandma?" Matthew asked.

"She's getting better. Slowly, but she's getting there." After another minute Carrie stood up, and Jonathan joined their cluster.

"Hi," he whispered, giving her a quick kiss on the lips before wrapping his arms around her and the kids.

"Hi back," she whispered with tears of gratitude filling her eyes.

"Don't cry Mommy," Katie said with a trembling lip.

"Aw, don't worry Katie. These are happy tears because it's so good to see you all!"

"I'll grab your stuff. You and the kids head inside. We were just about to have bedtime snacks."

"Ice cream Mommy! Daddy Johnny gives us *ice cream* for bedtime!"

"Seriously?" Carrie asked, but couldn't keep the smile off her face. Her kids were safe, healthy, and happy. She didn't care what they were eating before bed, as long as they were OK.

After Katie was in bed, Carrie, Jonathan, and Matthew sat at the table.

"So," Carrie started, "it's going to work out to have the wedding at my parent's church on Saturday. The doctor didn't think Mom would be home by then, but he said it's fine for her to attend the ceremony, and maybe even a bit of the reception. The church is fully accessible, so it will be easy for Dad and Mom."

"I don't get it."

"Get what, Matthew?"

"Well, you said the people in the church are bringing food for the reception. But how is it going to work? Don't they need a list or something? Shouldn't you be telling them what to do?"

She laughed and gave him a hug. He was so much like her—wanting to be organized and prepared. "If it's the way they used to do it, they'll organize it loosely according to last names. So, like those with last names from A-J will bring salads, and K-T will bring a main course, and the rest will bring dessert. Or something like that. It always seemed to work out! And honestly, I'm really pleased about us getting married there."

"And when your Grandma's better, the restaurant will reschedule the reception here, so we'll have another celebration!"

Carrie turned to Jonathan in surprise. She had assumed they'd lose their deposit and the booking since it was such late notice. "Honestly? Wow!"

"They wanted to do whatever they could for you. Hey, did you know they have a set of your colored frames in the hallway to the bathrooms?"

"What? No way! When did that happen?"

"No idea, but they look great! OK, back to the wedding stuff. So, Lisa will drive back here with the kids Saturday after the reception and she'll stay until we get back on Tuesday night."

"Should we maybe not go to Disneyland Mom?"

Carrie could tell Matthew desperately wanted to go but was trying to be mature about it.

"Well, I had a bit of a conversation with Grandma and Grandpa about that today. Basically Grandma said if we didn't go to Disneyland she'd get really sick and never recover."

"She was joking, right?" His eyebrows were furrowed together.

"Yeah, bud. That was a joke. But I do think knowing we're having a great time together will make her happy, and that will help her continue to get better. Plus, we can FaceTime her every day so she feels like she's part of all the magic."

"Cool!" he breathed, and his whole body sagged in relief.

After Matthew went to bed, Carrie and Jonathan sat on the couch together. He wrapped his arms around her and she settled into the security of his love. She was suddenly so tired...

"Carrie?" Jonathan whispered. His hand slowly stroked her arm. "Hey, Carrie?"

She struggled to remember where she was. Slowly she woke up enough to see she was in her living room, in Jonathan's arms.

"Hey there, I think you need to head to bed. You need some proper sleep."

"What? Oh, yeah, OK." She stood up and stumbled, and he quickly supported her. "Sorry," she mumbled.

"It's alright. I'll wait here until I see you in your room and then I'll let myself out and lock the door." He kissed her forehead. "Good night."

"Night."

CHAPTER 9

The week before her wedding was nothing like Carrie had planned. At least there wasn't any time for pre-wedding jitters, but worries about her mom and trying to catch up on everything filled her mind instead.

She went through the motions of her last two days at the women's center, barely registering all the nice things everyone said to her. Having Lauren there to paint and talk to the ladies was a huge help and allowed her to focus on the lessons that the different women took from Lauren's story. Everyone seemed impressed with Lauren and her approach to her life.

On Tuesday afternoon Dr. Bradley showed up to tell her she 'passed', and Carrie made sure all the clients had her contact information before she left. She used her mom's health as an excuse to avoid the conversation with Donna about continuing with the center on a volunteer basis—she just didn't have it in her to think about how much she wanted to keep helping the women, and how frustrating it was to work under Dr. Bradley.

She spent the evening trying to get last-minute preparations done, so they were ready for flying to Disneyland. There wouldn't be much time between coming home from the honeymoon and leaving the following day. At least she had grabbed some bigger summer clothes for the kids in August so they wouldn't be stuck wearing jeans and sweaters in California!

The spa day she planned for her and Jessica on Thursday had to be canceled. Instead, she called the lady who had always done their hair as little girls, and who still did her mom's hair. She was thrilled to come to her parent's house on Saturday to help them all get ready. There were a few times when Carrie fought tears of disappointment as the special things she planned for before the wedding would no longer happen.

On Wednesday, Carrie's last session at the clinic was with Megan and her mom. Janey noticed right away that Carrie had 'something up' and asked her about it. For a moment she debated brushing off the question but decided she could be real with them.

"Well, it's been a hard week. My mom was rushed to the hospital last week with a serious case of pneumonia, and it's been scary. She's going to be OK I think, but I was supposed to get married here in the city on Saturday, so in the middle of hospital visits and doctors we've been changing everything to get married in my hometown so my mom can be there."

"But you're still getting married, right?" Megan asked.

"Right. And you know, nothing else really matters. I'm still getting married. Everyone I'm really close to will still be there. So I'm good." She could give a genuine smile. "Thanks for asking about me. Now, tell me about the choices you two have been making since last week."

The session went by quickly. "You know, I'm really amazed at how you two are working so hard to change your thinking and the way you relate to each other. I can see a healthy new aspect to your relationship developing."

Megan smiled at her mom, "I think it's because we're both doing it. It makes everything easier when we're working on the same stuff."

"Well, I'm really pleased for both of you. As I said earlier, I'll be away for the next two Wednesdays, but I'll be back after that and I hope I can have another chance to chat with you both and hear how things are going."

After they left, Carrie sent off her last summary as an intern to Dr. Henshaw. She was excited to continue working at the clinic. Until her licensing came through they wouldn't pay much, but she had a long-term position and she was already looking forward to being back.

Kara was waiting for her when she stepped out of the office. "Alright soon-to-be-Mrs., everything ready?"

Carrie nodded. "I think so. I'm just going home to say goodbye to the kids and Jonathan and grab everything I need. Then I'll drive to Mom and Dad's to drop everything off before going to the hospital for the night. Either Jessica or my Dad will drive up here on Friday to pick up the kids, and then I'll see you all Saturday at the church. I'm exhausted just trying to keep track of it all."

Kara hugged her. "Remember, you deserve every good thing! Try to relax for these next few days. Oh, and get some sleep. Cause that man's not going to let you get much sleep!" She gave an exaggerated wink, and Carrie laughed.

"Right. Thanks for everything! See you soon!" She walked out of the clinic with a huge smile on her face. Only three more days until she was a married woman and she couldn't be happier. Knowing her mom wouldn't miss out on anything made it possible to look forward to the day.

Half an hour later she drove away from her house with tears in her eyes, and a promise to the kids that they would be picked up Friday as soon as school was out so they could have a sleepover at Grandma and Grandpa's before the wedding. The quiet during the drive gave her time to collect her thoughts. Everything had been so busy she hardly had any time to talk with Jonathan. And the talks they had were almost like business meetings—agreeing on times, last minute details, and making sure the kids' schedules were in order. Then Carrie would be so exhausted she'd head to bed.

All she knew was that he stayed up late every night trying to get his own work done before the weekend. She couldn't wait until their little honeymoon when they'd finally be able to focus on each other for three days.

When she got to the hospital, her sister and dad were sitting on a bench at the entrance waiting for her.

"You guys! It's cold out here! How long have you been waiting?" she said as she ran towards them.

Jessica quickly stood up, and the sisters met in a long bear hug. Again, Carrie started crying, but at least this time they were tears of joy. It was over a year since she had seen and hugged her little sister —too long!

She held Jessica back at arm's length to look at her but had to stop and wipe her eyes before her vision cleared. "Wow! You look stunning!" Jessica's auburn hair was styled into long, soft waves that seemed to make her green eyes stand out. Or maybe it was the skillfully applied makeup that Carrie could now see.

Jessica took a step back and twirled around. "It's my new image! A future partner's gotta look like money, you know?"

Everything about her shouted confidence and success, even though she was 'dressed down' in a black leather jacket, tight gray knit sweater, skinny jeans, and tall black boots.

"Well, you look amazing!" Carrie turned and hugged her dad, who was glowing with pride as he watched his two daughters. There were still circles under his eyes, but he looked like he'd gotten some rest and some food. "Hi Dad!"

"Hi Care Bear! Good to see you again. Now let's get you both inside and out of this wind!"

The girls wrapped arms around each other and walked in perfect sync into the hospital. Nurses and patients smiled and waved as they walked by.

"It feels like we're celebrities!" Carrie whispered.

"We are!" Jessica whispered back. "I'm a rock-star lawyer, and you're a super mom with a successful business and a hot fiancé! Doesn't get any better than that!"

They walked into their mom's room laughing, and her face brightened. "Oh, that's the best thing I've ever seen!"

Surrounding her bed, the little family hugged, and again Carrie's eyes filled with tears.

"What's with the waterworks?" Jessica demanded. "Are you pregnant or something?"

"Nope! Saving myself 'til Saturday night! But I'm just so emotional lately."

"It's because you've had so much going on! Between your practicum, and your wedding plans, and now me being sick—no wonder you need to let out a few emotions! You just need to keep letting it out and not stuffing it in."

Carrie smiled down at her mom. She was sitting up in bed wearing a new set of pajamas. Her hair looked freshly washed and styled, and the hollowness in her cheeks had vanished. "OK Mom. I'll do anything for you—as long as you promise to keep getting better."

"I have to! I need to get ready for having a son-in-law, and more grandbabies!" She turned to Jessica, "And I have to stick around for a long time to see this one settle down!"

"Settling down's overrated! Besides, Carrie's got the domestic thing down pat so I can be footloose and fancy free for a long time still."

They pulled up chairs brought in by a thoughtful nurse, and began to get caught up on wedding details, what the doctors had said, and Jessica's career.

"I just won a huge case last week. Actually, I was worried that it would carry into this week, but the jury was amazing. It's one of the firms' biggest awards so they really can't treat me like a rookie anymore."

"How's that going?" Carrie knew that Jessica constantly fought an exhausting combination of ageism, and an 'old boys club' mentality at the firm but she was determined to create space at the top for herself.

"Good! They're learning that I'm smarter than anyone else there, and I never give up a fight." She smirked. "And it helps to have new clients insisting on working with me."

"That's my girl!" their dad said with a huge smile. He had always tried to teach his girls they could do anything they dreamed of. Although his own dream of them both following in his footsteps as mechanics didn't work out, he figured they had still done pretty good for themselves.

CHAPTER 10

Later that night Carrie and Jessica sat on the couch in their child-hood home, feet curled up, mugs of hot chocolate warming their hands. Their mom insisted they all sleep in their own beds, and none of them wanted to argue with her. Carrie took the head nurse aside to make sure her mom was sleeping better, and he assured her that she had improved enough to let her sleep without having to check vitals throughout the night.

Already they could hear the gentle snores of their dad from the master bedroom.

Carrie giggled, "Maybe it was Dad's snoring keeping Mom up, not *her* coughing keeping *him* up!"

Jessica rolled her eyes, "If I was Mom I would've insisted on separate beds and a soundproof door!"

"I can't imagine that."

"Yeah. Me neither. Thank goodness she's getting better. He'd be lost without her."

"We're lucky they have each other. But I do think in the next few months we need to talk about them moving closer to Jonathan and I. That way we can keep an eye on Mom, and they can have better access to specialists."

"It's pretty easy, Carrie. Just get knocked up! Then they'll do anything for you!"

Carrie gently punched her sister's shoulder. "You're so cold about it!"

"Hey! I love your kids. And I'll love any more kids you have, promise!"

They sat there in silence as they both got lost in their thoughts. Carrie wished that Jessica could find the same sort of love that she had with Jonathan. But she also knew that Jessica loved what she did and the life she had. If a guy ever came along that she thought was worth some of the time she had left after work it would be a miracle.

"How are your finances? Were you OK with flying over and renting a car and everything?"

"You're kidding, right?"

"What?"

"Carrie, I'm making a snot load of money. And I never have time to spend any of it. So I *have* a snot load of money, and I'd pay anything to be here for your wedding."

"You've had time to buy some pretty amazing clothes! Did I tell you how fantastic you look? I mean, if this lawyer thing gets boring you should try modeling!"

A sad look crossed over Jessica's face before she forced a smile. "I don't buy my clothes. I use a shopping service. I mean, I really didn't have time to figure out where to go for new clothes anyway. So it's fine."

"Huh. So that part of the dream isn't quite working out?"

"Oh my gosh. Remember how I used to make lists of all the things I'd do when I had money?"

"I bet that journal is still in your room somewhere. But we both knew it all off by heart anyways." Carrie ticked things off on her fingers, "Get a swanky city apartment, buy gorgeous clothes, and take a vacation you had to get to by airplane every single year."

"Ah, the fantasies of youth! Well, I've got great clothes, that's one for the books. But I just haven't had the heart to move out of Mrs. Jacob's house. And it works fine to stay there. I'm pretty lucky, actually. Those homemade meals waiting for me at the end of every day always keep me going. Maybe one day I'll get my own place. But for now, I'm actually happy there."

"And the vacations? Why haven't you had one yet?"

"Are you kidding? When I have a day off the only thing I want to do is sleep. Mom worried that the hospital noises would keep me awake when I got here, but I was dead to the world. I can probably sleep through a rock concert at this point."

"I'm really proud of you, sis. It can't be easy to sacrifice everything like you've done."

"Whenever I start to feel sorry for myself, I just ignore it and focus on my clients. Nothing I'm going through compares to what they're going through—and will go through for the rest of their lives. That makes it all worth it."

A big yawn stopped Jessica from the sip of hot chocolate she was about to take.

"Speaking of sleep, I think you need some more, little sister."

"Not even gonna argue with you."

They both got up and took their mugs to the kitchen before hugging one more time and promising to talk more the next day.

Stretched out in the bed she had slept in since childhood, Carrie smiled into the darkness. There was something about knowing her sister was just on the other side of the wall that made her feel happy. Now she just needed the rest of her family nearby too. "Three more days," she whispered to herself before closing her eyes.

CHAPTER 11

Carrie was just about to text her sister to see when she'd arrive with the kids when the sound of Katie's voice traveled into the hospital room long before her body came through the door.

"Grandma! Grandpa! Mommy!" She ran to give each of them energetic hugs while talking a mile a minute, "Aunty Jessie took us to McDonald's and let us eat in her car! And it's a *fancy* car! And Daddy Johnny gave us ice cream every night, and Lisa and Jaz and baby Alex came over and brought the wedding dresses and they are *beeeautiful* Mommy! And mine is just like yours except there's lots more pink! And Alex can *walk*! Well, sorta walk. Like he can take a step and then he falls down, right on his bum!"

While she chattered, Matthew and Jessica followed her into the room and quietly hugged everyone. Laughing over Katie's monologue, they all settled onto the bed and the chairs. Nurses popped in and smiled at all the excitement, and Carrie noticed that all the patients walking past the open door had smiles on their faces too.

Already she regretted hanging onto the tradition of Jonathan not seeing her until the wedding. He should be here too! She quickly grabbed her phone and FaceTimed him.

"Hey gorgeous!" he said with a face-splitting smile.

"Hey yourself! I wanted to include you in the reunion." She panned her phone across the noisy group, giving everyone time to say hello to him.

"Take good care of my bride everyone! I'll be early to the ceremony, in case she wants to start sooner than two!"

The all laughed and promised to deliver her to the church on time—if not earlier—before he excused himself to get back to work.

"Oh! I wanted to bring Mom's dress in for you all to see! Hang on!" Jessica got up and hurried out of the room. On her way back they could hear the nurses' exclamations as she walked past.

"Ta da!" she shouted with a dramatic pose that held the dress up for everyone to see.

The women gasped collectively, and the father-of-the-bride chuckled. "Well, it's almost as beautiful as you are, dear!"

"Oh, you!" she replied with a smile, and flapped her hand at him.

The dress looked like a Monet painting with gorgeous swirls of blues, greens, and whites. It was obviously carefully tailored to flatter, and looked incredibly comfortable.

"Mom, Dad will have to take you out on a bunch of hot dates to get your use out of this!" Jessica quipped.

Carrie agreed, "This has to be more than a once-in-a-lifetime dress, Mom. It's perfect for you. Jaz is a miracle worker. Wait till you see our dresses, right Katie?"

Katie giggled, "Right!"

Her dad turned to Matthew, "And what will you be wearing young man?"

Matthew smiled shyly, "Jonathan and I are renting gray suits and we have matching bow ties. He said when I'm not growing so fast, we'll go and buy suits. The lady at the shop had to make the legs on mine longer because I grew since she measured me!"

"I think you've grown since last week! Must be all that ice cream Jonathan feeds you!" Carrie's heart felt full of pride for her kids. The times away from them last week and this week were the longest she'd ever been away, and while a part of her heart hurt when she was gone, she was also relieved that they seemed OK. She hoped she wouldn't miss them too much on her honeymoon. But thank goodness Lisa could stay with them on short notice.

"What's the smile for Care Bear?"

Carrie turned to her mom in surprise. "Oh! Sorry, I didn't realize I was smiling!"

"Sorry you're smiling, or sorry for *why* you're smiling?" Jessica asked with a wink.

"What do you mean Aunty Jessie?"

"Well, the thing is Katie—"

"—Stop!" Carrie said laughing, "Let's just say I'm happy because I have such a wonderful life, OK?"

"OK Mommy. Aunty Jessie said we're going to get our hair and nails done tomorrow! I've never had that stuff before!"

"She's right! One of Grandma's friends is going to come to the house and get us all done up for the wedding!"

"And the men in the house are going out for a big pancake breakfast so we can have a break from all the chaos you ladies will create," her dad said, looking at Matthew.

"*I* can go?"

"Don't see any other men around! It's just you and me against the world kiddo."

"Oh puh-lease!" Jessica said.

Matthew smiled big and turned to his mom. "What's for supper?"

"Supper? You just ate McDonald's an hour ago!" Jessica protested.

"That was a snack!"

"Your Grandma and I have it all figured out. But it's a surprise. So you'll have to wait another hour."

Matthew opened his mouth to protest and then shut it quickly when he saw his mom's stern look. "OK," he said meekly.

The nurse bustled in with a clipboard and a blood pressure machine on a pole with wheels.

"Should we step out?" Carrie asked.

"No way! I can work around you all. Plus, I'm sure her blood pressure's better when she's got all of you so close by. I just need to take a set of vitals and then we'll leave you alone until bedtime."

"What's vitals?" Katie asked.

The nurse proceeded to carefully explain everything she was doing to a wide-eyed Katie. There wasn't a single question the nurse couldn't answer, and the rest of the people in the room found themselves learning along with her. The last thing she did was transfer her patient into her wheelchair. When she left, Katie turned to her mom with a serious face.

"That's what I'm gonna do when I'm big."

"What? Answer a second grader's questions?"

"No! Be a nurse and make grandmas feel better!"

Her grandma reached out and cupped her cheek. "Oh Katie, you'll make a lovely nurse. In fact, I'm feeling better already, just cause you're here!"

"You are?" she asked wide-eyed.

"Definitely!"

They continued to visit until a phone buzzed.

"Oh, that's mine. Excuse me." Carrie's dad quickly swiped at his phone and left the room. Five minutes later he was back. "Dinner's this way! Follow the old people!" He wheeled her mom out of the room and down the hallway. A few turns led them to a small meeting room decked out in bright streamers. The mouth-watering smells of Mexican food were already wafting into the hallway.

"Welcome to your last dinner as a single woman, Care Bear!"

Carrie stopped in surprise. "How on earth did you manage this? Oh my gosh. I'm suddenly so hungry!"

"We figured you'd be craving all your favorites, so Marcos and Glenda helped us plan a little dinner, and the nurses pulled off some quick decorating." The owners of the local Mexican restaurant were well known for their delicious food, and Carrie couldn't wait to dig in.

"Awesome," Matthew breathed as they all found places at the table. Soon everyone had their plates filled with enchiladas, quesadillas, carnitas, and flautitas.

When the adults had eaten their fill, they continued to visit and joke with Matthew, who was still eating. Carrie happily let Katie onto her lap and enjoyed having her daughter in close contact again.

"OK, so I dropped off your wedding clothes at the house before we came here. And Mrs. Macintosh will be at the house by nine to start on hair and makeup," Jessica said, dipping another tortilla chip into the pico de gallo.

"Do I get makeup too, Mommy?" Katie asked, sitting up and turning to face her mom.

"Just a little bit!"

"YAY!"

"Is there anything that needs taking care of at the church still? I feel like I've been right out of it, lying in that hospital bed."

Carrie smiled across the table at her mom, "The most important thing is you feeling well enough to come! Mrs. Leung said there was nothing left to do when I called her yesterday. They set up tables in the meeting hall and just used the regular white table clothes. And the ladies from the coffee group will take care of making coffee and tea and cleaning up afterward. So, as long as the groom gets to the church on time we're good!"

Matthew sighed and pushed his plate back a little.

"Did you finally get enough to eat?" Jessica asked with a grin.

"Yeah. That was pretty good." He paused and looked around the room. "So, um, aren't weddings supposed to be super stressful and stuff? I mean, one of my friends at school, her mom got married this summer, and she was telling me it would be the worst month of my life!"

Carrie laughed, "Well, most weddings are way more work than mine, that's for sure. But Jonathan and I just wanted to keep it simple. And we're super lucky that the church here could accommodate us on such short notice—that's a small town thing, you know, everyone happy to pitch in, and all the ladies in the church know how to operate the coffee maker!"

"Some of us men do, too!" her Dad protested.

"Why didn't you plan it for here at the start then?"

Carrie smiled and rolled her eyes. "Good question! I didn't even think of it! So bud, any chance you'll want this food for a midnight snack, or should we just toss the leftovers?"

"Ha ha," he replied.

"What? What's the joke?" Jessica asked.

"Leftovers are always his last meal of the day," Carrie explained.

"Good thing I can afford more groceries now, because every day needs a new meal with this guy around."

"I can't help it!" Matthew weakly protested, with a smile on his face. Every once in a while, he still asked Carrie if they had enough money to pay for all the food he ate. He was always relieved that his appetite didn't hurt the family budget.

CHAPTER 12

"Good morning little miss bride!"

A sing songy voice interrupted Carrie's sleep, and she struggled to open her eyes. "What? What's going on?" Slowly the outline of Jessica came into view and Carrie could see she was carrying a tray with a coffee mug and a single rose in a vase.

"Well, you've got to start the day off on the right foot!" Jessica explained, setting the tray on the night table. "After all, you'll need lots of energy for today—and tonight!" With a grin she walked out of the room, closing the door behind her.

Carrie sat up and reached for the mug, enjoying the aroma of freshly brewed coffee for a moment before taking her first sip. She rested her head back against the wall with a sigh. Matthew started bringing her coffee in bed for Mother's Day a few years ago, but it was definitely a luxury she could get used to. And she appreciated that Jessica insisted Katie have a 'sleepover' in Aunty's room and that she knew to let her have a little time alone to wake up and think about the day.

It had taken a while to fall asleep. She worked through a variety of anti-anxiety strategies as worries about her wedding night and married life kept overtaking her thoughts. Even though she knew Jonathan was a completely different man than her first husband, the lingering wounds from her last marriage hadn't all healed.

At least she when she fell asleep she didn't have any nightmares. They were much less frequent than they had been, and she was grateful that part of her was moving past her fears about Don. Now she was determined to enjoy every moment of her wedding day, and hopefully the night, too. After finishing her coffee she stretched and closed her eyes for a few minutes of her favorite meditation of repeating 'I love myself', before grabbing the tray and making her way out of her room.

Katie and Matthew were already at the table where Jessica had set out muffins, fruit, yogurt, and granola.

"I wasn't sure how you'd feel about eating this morning, but Matthew promises me he can eat what's left after he goes out for breakfast!"

"This looks great, Jess. Thanks!" She gave each of her kids a hug and a kiss on the forehead. "How are you feeling about today Matthew?"

"Good. I'm glad we'll finally be a real family. And I can't wait to see what the food is."

Katie wiggled in her seat, trying to stay quiet until she was asked. As soon as Carrie looked at her and smiled, the words burst out, "I'm SOOOO excited Mommy because today I get to wear my prettiest dress ever, and carry flowers, and Daddy Johnny has a special present for me! Do you know what it is Mommy?"

Carrie tried to remember Jonathan saying something about a gift, but she came up blank. "I have no idea Katie-girl. I guess we'll all be surprised!"

"And how's my favorite family today?" Carrie's dad asked as he walked into the room.

"Grandpa!" Katie giggled, "We're your *only* family!"

"Still my favorite!" He declared before opening his arms for hugs from his grandchildren. Katie and Matthew willingly went over for hugs while Carrie and Jessica looked on, smiling.

We need to be together more often, Carrie thought.

"Alright Matthew. I think we'd better get out of here before we're caught between curling irons and make-up brushes." He gave an exaggerated shudder before picking up his keys. Matthew followed him out without a glance back.

Carrie felt a moment of sadness that her mom couldn't be there to join them before hearing a pinging sound coming from the table. Jessica picked up the iPad.

"Good morning Care Bear!" her mom said from the screen.

"Mom! I was just starting to feel sad that you couldn't join us for breakfast!"

"Well, I can't smell your coffee, but I can smell mine, so that's pretty close to perfect." She held up a hospital mug in a toast to her daughters and Jessica and Carrie raised theirs in response.

"Me too Grandma!" Katie said loudly, lifting her glass of orange juice.

They ate and chatted happily. When a knock at the door signaled the arrival of the hairdresser, they rearranged the iPad so she could continue to be a part of the day.

With the sound of happy voices around her, and the knowledge that soon she'd see Jonathan again, Carrie relaxed and enjoyed a rare morning of pampering. She decided to style her hair in a classic French twist, with soft curls framing her face.

Jessica and Katie were both wearing their hair down, and Katie had two sparkly pink barrettes that would keep her brown curls off her face.

When the men returned from breakfast, everyone was getting final touches done on their makeup, and Jessica was doing Katie's nails.

"Well, aren't you all the picture of prettiness!" After kissing his daughters and admiring Katie's nails, Carrie's dad excused himself to go get ready.

"You can change in my bedroom Matthew," Jessica offered. Matthew had slept on the couch in the living room overnight.

"And then you and Katie need to make sure all your stuff is packed up," Carrie added. "I think Lisa's taking you home straight from the church so put everything in Aunty's car when you're ready."

"Mommy, are you and Daddy Johnny still going on your honeycomb thing?" Katie asked without taking her eyes off her newly painted fingernails.

"You mean our honey*moon*?"

"Yes! That thing!"

"We are! Thanks to Lisa coming to stay with you. We'll be back in time to pick you up from school on Tuesday, and then on Wednesday we all fly to Disneyland!"

"YAY!" Katie shouted, flapping her hands in the air while her nail polish dried. "And I can show Minnie Mouse my pretty nails! I'll bet she likes them!"

When Matthew walked out of the bedroom with his suit on, Carrie struggled to find any words. Her little boy walked into the bedroom, and a young man walked out. He had carefully styled his hair, his suit fit perfectly, and even his bow tie was picture-perfect.

"Matthew! You're one stylin' man!" Jessica walked over and held her hand up for a high five.

"Thanks! Jonathan and I YouTube'd how to tie these things so we could get it right." He shifted a little. "It feels cool to wear this! I can't wait 'til I'm done growing so I can have my own!"

"You look amazing son, and your outside look matches your fantastic heart."

He smiled shyly, "Thanks, Mom."

With Carrie's makeup done and Katie's nails dry, they went to get dressed.

"Oh Mommy!" Katie breathed after Jessica zipped up the back of Carrie's dress, "You're like the perfectest princess *ever*."

Carrie didn't have many princess moments in her memory, but this was definitely one of them. She stood in front of the mirror, shocked at what she saw. The proverbial broke single mom of a few years ago was gone forever. In its place was a magical vision better than she could ever have imagined.

Her hair and makeup somehow made her eyes shine and her lips sparkle. From the elegant line of her neck where a simple pearl neck-lace rested, her gaze dropped to a hint of cleavage highlighted by the chiffon band that wrapped around her shoulders. The bodice clung to her and made her waist look much smaller than she thought it was, before curving around her hips and falling gracefully to the floor.

She turned a little and let her leg slide out past the slit. The saucy finish to the elegant dress was exactly what she wanted—a not-so-subtle hint that she was still young-at-heart and ready to have some fun.

"That's it," Jessica declared. "You better take real good care of this dress missy, because if I ever get married, I'm wearing it. Dear Lord Carrie, did you even warn Jonathan? The poor man's going to die of a heart attack before he even makes it to the wedding night!"

"What?" Katie wailed, "Daddy Johnny's going to die?"

Jessica dropped to her knees and faced Katie, "No way, girl! That's just an expression to mean your Mommy's so beautiful that Daddy Johnny's going to love it!"

"Oh. Why didn't you just say that?"

There was a knock at the door, "Everything OK in there, girls?"

With a nod from Carrie, Jessica opened the door. As soon as he saw her, Carrie's dad pulled out a tissue.

"Oh, my dear girl. You are as beautiful as your mom was the day she married me."

"Mom! Where's Mom?" Jessica hollered.

"I'll bring her!" Matthew called back. He ran into the room with the iPad and stopped short. "Whoa Mom! You look crazy good! Here…" He lifted up the iPad and flipped the view so Carrie's mom could get her first look at her daughter.

"Oh Care Bear," she said through her tears, "this is such a special moment. I love you so much and I'm so happy you've been brave enough to find this life you have now. You deserve every good thing that's coming your way."

Carrie blinked quickly and tried to stop the tears before her makeup got ruined, "Thanks, Mom. And thanks to all of you. I'm so blessed to have such an amazing family. And I know Jonathan's so excited to officially have a family to call his own. And I'm going to stop now before we all start bawling and wreck this perfect make-up."

They switched to lighter topics, grateful that Carrie's mom could join them, even if it was over a screen, while Carrie's mind wandered to her soon-to-be-husband. Jonathan lost his parents in a car accident a few years ago, and he'd admitted to Carrie that he still sometimes struggled with overwhelming grief over their deaths.

They had set aside two chairs at the front row of the church that held signs remembering Jonathan's parents. Those seats would remain empty for the ceremony, except for a bouquet of pink roses — Jonathan's mom's favorite — that Jenny had thoughtfully ordered. Carrie knew it would be bittersweet to get married without his parents there to celebrate.

CHAPTER 13

Carrie's dad left to go pick up her mom from the hospital, and the rest of them got into Jessica's rental car for the drive to the church. When they got to the back of the church, she could hardly breathe for all the excitement and nerves.

"Mom? Are you OK?" Matthew was turned around in the front passenger seat, looking at her.

"Uh, I guess I'm excited. And nervous." She looked up and met her sister's sympathetic gaze in the rearview mirror.

"Why are you nervous, Mommy?" Katie reached over and touched the chiffon on Carrie's arm. "Princesses are happy, not nervous!"

"I guess this princess needs to be happy then! Are you ready to go get yourself a Daddy?"

Katie nodded confidently, and Matthew and Jessica got out and opened the doors for them. Jessica helped Carrie get out without brushing her dress on the car and they made their way into the side entrance of the church where they settled into a little room.

A few minutes later her parents came in. Her mom had a bright smile, her hair was done beautifully, and the dress complimented her pale skin. Carrie let out a breath of relief that she didn't realize she was holding to see her mom well enough to attend her wedding. A 'pop' sound made them all turn around. Jessica had somehow snuck a bottle of prosecco and four crystal glasses in with her.

"Jessica!" their mom admonished, "I don't think you should be serving us alcohol in the church!"

A mischievous smile flashed across her face—one the rest of them remembered well from her childhood. "I'm pretty sure I can do whatever I want. And we're going to take this little moment to celebrate before Carrie goes and gets herself hitched."

They toasted their health, happiness, and Carrie's new love. As the bubbles tickled her mouth, Carrie felt some of the nervousness leave her body. With her family around her, and knowing that Jonathan and her friends were close by, she started to feel like everything would be OK.

Carrie's dad looked at his watch. "I think it's time for Matthew to take Grandma out. There's a spot right at the very front row for the chair. You'll see it."

Matthew smiled. "OK, and then I can sit beside her until you bring Mom down, right Grandpa?"

"It's a good thing you're not a bridezilla!" Jessica laughed, "Because we're all winging it here!"

"Aunty Jessica, when's it our turn?"

She crouched down beside Katie, "As soon as Matthew and Grandma are settled. You ready?"

Katie nodded.

"Oh, wait! We need pictures!"

Carrie and Jessica both rolled their eyes at their mom, and then Carrie admitted it was a good thing she mentioned it! After taking just enough pictures to satisfy, they were ready. The pastor's wife popped her head in, complimented them all on how beautiful they looked, and then announced that it was time to begin.

Carrie tucked her arm into her dad's and smiled at him.

"Well Care Bear," her dad started, "this is the beginning of a new life, isn't it?"

Carrie nodded, afraid that speaking would start her eyes tearing up again.

When they received the signal to go ahead Carrie and her dad exchanged smiles, and began their walk towards the door that would open into the sanctuary. Her last thought as a single mom was that she was walking towards her own personal sanctuary—Jonathan.

The doors opened, and the strains of a classical guitar wafted over Carrie. Following her Dad's lead, she began to walk down the aisle. There were so many glowing faces standing to greet her that she didn't see Jonathan at first. She registered people from her child-hood and new friends she had made in the past few years. Then, movement at the front of the church caught her eye as Jonathan took a half step forward and entered her vision.

A gasp escape her lips as she took in the man she was about to marry. He stood tall and proud at the front of the church with a huge smile and cheeks glistening with tears. His grey suit fit his broad shoulders perfectly and the blue bow tie seemed to reflect the clear blue in his eyes.

Carrie felt her dad stop a step away and reluctantly stopped beside him.

"Who gives this woman to be married to this man?" Pastor Leung asked in a clear, kind voice.

"Her mother and I do," her dad answered in a shaky voice.

Carrie turned to kiss him on the cheek and caught a glimpse of Jonathan leaning over to kiss her mom on the cheek before turning to her dad. The two men shook hands with tears in their eyes, and then he turned to Carrie and reached out his hand. He opened his mouth to say something, but his chin began to tremble and he quickly closed his mouth.

Carrie slipped her right hand into his, and with her left hand reached up and softly wiped his tears away. A gentle laugh rippled through the guests and a sense of love and happiness seemed to be floating around them.

Together Carrie and Jonathan walked the two steps toward the pastor and then turned to face each other. They reached out and joined both hands as the music faded and then stopped. Looking into Jonathan's eyes, Carrie felt a balm of healing soothe her heart. In that moment, she knew that the worst of the wounds from the past could now heal.

After a brief message, the Pastor turned to Jonathan, "You've prepared your own vows, so this is your time to share with your bride and these witnesses your commitment from this day forward."

Jonathan's chin trembled again, and he took a deep breath before starting, "Carrie, I can honestly say that the first time I saw you, you took my breath away. In fact, you left me speechless. And now I'm afraid that all the words in the world aren't enough to tell you what you mean to me. My heart was hard and cold, but somehow you made it beat again. Your courage to live each day looking for the best in people, and your willingness to accept me into your life are beyond what I can understand.

"From the way you are such an amazing mom to Matthew and Katie, to the way you care for your family, your friends, and your clients, you are everything good that I've wished for in my life. I commit that every day from now on I will cherish you, love you, and support you. I will even ask for forgiveness every time I screw up!"

Everyone chuckled, and Carrie smiled softly at him.

"I'll be there for you no matter what," he continued. "I'll do my best to help you raise Matthew and Katie and show them how much love

I have for them, and for their mom. No matter what happens, in sickness, in health, richer, poorer, and beyond death, I will love you with my whole being."

Carrie felt overwhelmed by his commitment to her and the amount of love obvious in every word he said. She paused, trying to compose herself before she began her own vows, but Jonathan let go of her right hand and turned slightly towards her family.

"Matthew and Katie, this is the part I talked to you about earlier."

To her surprise, both kids stood up and came to stand beside Carrie, with Katie holding both her hand and Matthew's hand. She looked at Jonathan and raised an eyebrow, but he just smiled before turning his attention to the kids.

"The only thing better than the first day I met your mom was meeting you two."

Carrie could hear sniffles coming from the audience and she felt her own eyes tearing up again.

Jonathan reached out and took Matthew's hand, and suddenly they were a perfect circle. "It's clear to me that everything good that's in your mom is in you two as well. Every day I learn more from you two about the best job in the world. Do you know what that job is?"

"It's being Daddy Johnny!" Katie announced triumphantly, and the emotional tension broke as everyone burst out laughing.

"You're absolutely right Katie. Now, I'm kind of late to the Daddy job, but I promise both of you that I will do my best every day to be the dad that you deserve. I am *so proud* that I get to call myself your dad, and I will be here for you no matter what from this day until forever. I love you both!"

Carrie suddenly wanted her kids beside her for the rest of the ceremony. She squeezed Katie's hand and mouthed *stay here* to both kids.

The Pastor turned to her with a huge smile on his face, "Carrie, if you're able to speak after that incredible moment, I believe you have your own vows."

Carrie nodded and took a deep breath, "Phew! I thought I felt like the luckiest woman in the world walking down the aisle a few moments ago, but I believe this just surpassed that moment. Jonathan, I made it clear to you that I wasn't looking for a relationship when we first met. But you never gave up on me—or on us. You've believed in us with an unwavering conviction that helped me learn to trust in love.

"You've accepted me and the kids without reservation, and your love for us is like a fresh dose of healing every day. I promise to give you my whole heart and all my love every day. I will remain true to you, not just on the outside, but from the center of my soul. I will walk beside you, love you, accept you, and forgive you every time you need forgiving." She winked at him, and everyone burst out laughing.

"You are my heart and my soul, and I give you myself, in sickness and health, richer or poorer, for the rest of forever."

They exchanged wedding bands, and Carrie gently touched the colorful band that sparkled and shone back at her. It was Jonathan's idea to have a band made with gems in every color to match her personality and her love for bright colors. She looked up at him, ready for the kiss to seal their vows, but Jonathan turned away and nodded to his brother Max who quickly stood up and walked over to their little group. Max took out a jewelry box and opened it, allowing Jonathan to take a chain out.

Jonathan cleared his throat, holding the chain between two shaking hands. Carrie could see a golden eagle at the end of it. "Matthew, for your entire life you have been looking out for your mom and sister, protecting them, and doing everything you can to make their life better. I know you will continue to do this, and I support the powerful role you've given yourself. That's the first part of what this necklace represents. But from now on, *I* will watch over *you*. I will protect you, I will fight for you, and I will do everything *I* can to make *your* life better. This is my promise to you."

Matthew stepped forward and Jonathan put the necklace on him. They solemnly shook hands before Matthew spontaneously reached out and enveloped Jonathan in a hug. Everyone responded with sighs and more tears.

Jonathan turned for the second necklace, and Max handed it to him before quietly going back to his seat. The necklace had a rainbow of gems that seemed to match Carrie's wedding band.

"Katie, you are unlike anyone I have ever known. Your tornado of excitement and love is one of the best things anyone can experience, and I'm lucky to be caught up in it. I promise to be everything a Daddy Johnny should be. I will love you, protect you, buy you games, take you to all the activities you love to do, and listen to you carefully every day."

He kneeled and carefully put the necklace on her before giving her the tiniest kiss on her cheek. Katie, in a perfect copy of her mom, reached up and wiped away the tear that rolled down his cheek.

"Is that a happy tear Daddy?" she whispered. He nodded, and they both shared a smile before he stood up.

Jessica leaned forward and whispered for the kids to come back and sit with her, and Carrie and Jonathan turned to face each other.

The pastor prayed a blessing over the couple before smiling and adding, "And now, you may kiss your bride."

Carrie felt her breath catch for a minute as Jonathan reached up and cradled her face in his hands. Her last thought before she closed her eyes was that everything would be OK. Seconds—or maybe minutes—later she was vaguely aware of cheers coming from the audience as their kiss slowly ended.

They signed the register with Max and Jessica as witnesses and then stood side by side at the front of the church.

"Ladies and gentlemen," the pastor announced, "It is my immense pleasure to present to you Mr. and Mrs. Brandt."

Everyone jumped up and cheered as the newlyweds walked down the aisle. The people were a blur of colorful support to Carrie. All she could think about was how she never wanted Jonathan to let go of her.

CHAPTER 14

The reception became a community celebration of Jonathan, Carrie, Carrie's family, and Carrie's mom's recovery. Jessica ran interference long enough to make sure Carrie and Jonathan got a chance to eat before letting the crowd loose on them.

About half an hour later, Carrie's dad pulled them aside. "I think it's time for your mom to head back to the hospital. Can we have a few minutes?"

They moved to the entrance where the few people there gave them some privacy. Jonathan kneeled down beside the wheelchair and took Carrie's Mom's hand. "I hoped we'd have more time to get to know each other before the wedding, but I want you to know that I'll treasure your daughter and your grandchildren for the rest of my days. And I hope that I can be an important part of your family."

Carrie's mom patted his hand and smiled at him. "I couldn't wish for a better husband for Carrie or a better dad for the kids. And I hope you'll think of us as your bonus parents from now on. We love you like a son, my dear."

His eyes filled with tears. "Thanks Mom," he whispered. When he stood up, Carrie's dad was ready to hug him.

"Took Carrie long enough, but we finally got a real son out of this parenting deal!" he joked. Together they laughed, hugged, and wiped away tears.

"Now, I don't want to hear anything from you for the next three days! Your dad and I will be just fine. And as soon as I'm better we'll come stay in that lovely house of yours."

Carrie reached down for a final hug, "OK Mom. I love you. Just wait here a sec and I'll go find the kids to say goodbye."

A few minutes later, Carrie, Jonathan, Matthew, and Katie were all waving goodbye. Turning around, Carrie nearly ran into Jaz, standing behind her with Maria, Lisa, Jenny, Kara, and Lauren.

Kara stepped forward. "We need to step into another room for some important business with Carrie."

"Can I come too?" Katie asked.

Lauren kneeled down, "Trust me, honey, you do not want to be part of this. But could you maybe go help Dustin with Brittany? She's driving him nuts!"

Katie's face immediately brightened. "OK!" She turned and ran back into the hall where the hum of voices and the clatter of cutlery against plates continued.

Carrie gave Jonathan and Matthew a questioning look and followed her friends into the nearest Sunday School classroom.

"OK," Kara started once they were all sitting around a table with the door firmly closed behind them, "We had a fun little surprise bridal shower planned, but your schedule changed with your mom being sick. So, we thought the best thing was to bring the shower to you today! And this gives us all a few minutes to spend with you before you're off."

"You guys!" Carrie protested. "You really didn't need to!" She noticed that everyone was carrying a gift bag.

"Oh, we really think we did!" Lauren argued with a huge smile on your face. "I bet you didn't exactly take time to shop for your honeymoon, so we did it for you!"

"Wha..." She couldn't think of what to say to that. She *had* planned to pick out some lingerie, but with everything that had happened in the last week she hadn't had a chance. "You don't even know my size!"

"Not true! I know your exact size!" Jaz reminded her. "And now everyone else does too!" she giggled.

"We'd better get going on this before Jonathan bursts through the door and drags Carrie away!" Jenny added.

Carrie took a big breath and started opening gifts. Somehow, her friends mostly picked things she loved, and that suited her. And she might even try out the more risqué things that she would *never* have considered buying!

Ten minutes later she was still blushing like a young bride but felt overwhelmed that she had such thoughtful friends who knew her so well.

"So, how do I get these into Jonathan's car?"

"Leave that to me!" Jenny offered. "Here, we'll put everything into this gift bag, and I'll pop it in the car just before you head off. After all, it's really a gift for Jonathan too!" she winked.

They all went back into the hall and Carrie quickly made her way back to Jonathan's side. He gave Carrie a questioning look, but she just smiled at him and turned to Max and Dustin who he'd been talking with.

Carrie was grateful she shared the same circle of friends with her husband. Being with them created another safe place for her, and it meant a lot that they were all here to celebrate two of their friends getting married. She briefly wondered if Lauren and Dustin would ever tie the knot before they were interrupted by Katie trying to keep up with Brittany.

"She's really fast now!" she gasped to Dustin.

He nodded and gave both girls a lopsided smile. Dustin was still working on re-learning skills he lost after a drug overdose several years earlier, and now he could speak in three and four word-sentences if he didn't rushed. "My little runner!" he said slowly and proudly. He reached out a hand and Brittany reluctantly took hold. Carrie knew from experience she'd stay there until her dad let her go and she marveled at the control he had with his toddler.

Jonathan's arm reached around her waist, and he leaned closer. "Are you ready to get going Mrs. Brandt?" he whispered. Shivers trickled down her spine as she nodded. She was definitely ready.

CHAPTER 15

The sound of everyone cheering for the new couple faded as Jonathan drove away. Carrie shifted a little so she could see his profile. He turned and gave her a huge smile before facing the road again.

"I couldn't have asked for a more perfect day," he admitted. "I really didn't think it mattered where or how we got married, but being able to go back to your hometown with the people who have known you your whole life was great!"

He reached across and touched her cheek. "And you just keep taking my breath away with your beauty! I am the luckiest man on the planet."

Carrie looked down for a minute before looking back at him. "Thanks," she whispered. For the moment she couldn't think of anything else to say. She desperately wanted to mark every second of this day into her memory but a part of her struggled to believe it was real.

They drove in silence as a perfect sunset left a blend of pinks across the sky. "I hope Katie gets to see this!" Jonathan said. "She'll be convinced God painted the sky just for her!"

"When did you get those necklaces? And how did you think of that?"

"Uh, I'd like to say it was my own brilliant idea, but I spent a bunch of time Googling blended families and stuff for ideas. I wanted them to be a part of the ceremony too, so they'd know how much they mean to me."

"It was perfect. Thank you."

"Hey, I'm the lucky one here. I get *you* as my wife and two amazing kids all in one day. I never dreamed things could turn out like this for me. No matter what else comes, Carrie, this is everything to me."

"So... what can you tell me about where we're staying?" She felt like she needed to lighten the mood before they both started crying. Even if they were tears of joy, there really shouldn't be that many tears on a wedding day!

"Have you heard of the Waite Inn?"

"Just a little bit. That's the former mansion on the edge of the city that's a luxury inn... Seriously? We're going there?" Carrie couldn't picture herself staying somewhere so elegant.

"Not exactly..." he smiled as she exhaled in relief. "They've restored the groundskeeper's cottage, and that's where we're booked for the weekend. I didn't get to see it in person, but one of my clients who stayed there recommended it."

When they drove up the gently curving road leading to the main building, Carrie took in the scenery with a gaping mouth. The majestic pine trees lining both sides were softly lit from below, creating a border of light and shadow that felt surreal.

The towering wooden columns that supported the grand entryway were balanced by millions of fairy lights throughout the greenery in the front and along a veranda that wrapped around the inn. Tall windows let out a warm glow and gave glimpses of the luxury waiting inside.

Jonathan slowed as they approached the front of the inn, and a man in a dark suit walked from the entrance to the car.

"Good evening Mr. and Mrs. Brandt. Congratulations on your wedding! We're all ready for you. Please follow the lane to the left around the inn until you come to the cottage. A staff member is there to assist you with your luggage."

Jonathan thanked him and followed the lane that was just visible as they came to it. It turned away from the inn almost immediately and wound through the trees until the cottage came into view. Made entirely of stone, the single story building had its own wrap around porch and a single spot for parking to the side.

As soon as Jonathan parked the car a middle-aged woman in a suit opened Carrie's door. "Good evening Mrs. Brandt. Welcome to Waite Cottage, and congratulations!"

Carrie thanked her and stepped out of the car. She was glad she was still in her wedding dress to walk into such a beautiful setting. Jonathan joined her, and together they walked through the ornately carved door into the cottage. A fire in the stone fireplace set the mood in the living area, where overstuffed chairs invited them to relax and forget the outside world. The décor was a blend of country comforts and modern elegance. Carrie tried to take in all the little touches—candles flickering, a champagne bottle in an ice bucket with two crystal flutes on the table beside, and feathery soft blankets draped over the chairs.

"I'll give you a short tour, and help with your luggage," the lady quietly said. There was a fully stocked kitchen with a plate of cheese and fruit already set on the counter, a master bedroom with a spa-like bathroom and more candles, and a hot tub on the back porch overlooking the forest. "Should you need anything at all, just pick up the phone and dial 'one', or you can text the main desk. Otherwise, you're completely private here and we won't disturb you. You're welcome to join us in the dining room for breakfast tomorrow, or we can bring it to you here."

Jonathan followed her out to the car to collect their luggage, and Carrie went over to stand in front of the fireplace. The warmth calmed the goosebumps that had shown up on the walk inside, and she breathed in the subtle smell of pine.

Just before they were alone, the lady deftly opened the champagne and poured two glasses. With a smile and a reminder to contact the front desk if they needed anything, she was gone.

Jonathan handed Carrie a glass and picked up the other one.

"To love, to us, and to our family," he said as his eyes shone.

"Cheers," Carrie whispered as she took a sip.

CHAPTER 16

They spent a blissful 24 hours together hidden away in the cottage before deciding to venture down to the inn for dinner at the restaurant. Everything they could wish for was at hand, and they enjoyed the meals brought right to their doorstep whenever they felt like eating.

When they emerged from their private world, Carrie happily brought out a long-sleeved deep blue dress that seemed too dressy when she was quickly packing. In this setting it was just right. Jonathan decided to pass on the jeans and dress shirt he planned to wear and put on his wedding suit instead.

After a few minutes of noticing all the other elegantly dressed diners, Carrie relaxed. The setting might be luxurious, but the service was welcoming, and the food was the best she had ever tasted. They lingered over decaf coffees before declining the offer of a ride back to the cottage in one of the inn's golf carts.

Walking back, hand-in-hand, Carrie leaned into Jonathan. "I keep on feeling like I've been transported to another world."

He wrapped his arm around her waist, "I know what you mean. But it's real. And we're really here together. And we still have all day tomorrow and part of Tuesday before shifting to the magical world of Mr. Disney!"

They took advantage of the uninterrupted time to get to know each other in every way. Carrie continuously delighted in finding ways that they were compatible, or somehow complemented each other perfectly.

Her favorites times were the mornings when Jonathan would slip out of bed and bring back mugs of the best coffee she had ever tasted while they indulged in long, lazy mornings. They talked about every-thing—Jonathan's memories of his parents, Carrie's life as a care-giver to her mom, and all the things they were just discovering about each other.

Carrie's worries about being intimate were quickly dispelled. "I am *so* glad we didn't postpone the honeymoon!" she laughed as they sat side by side in the kitchen for a late-night snack.

"Well, we *could* have made it work..."

Seeing the twinkle in his eye she got up and came around the rustic table. Wiggling into his lap, she began kissing him. "Really?" she whispered against his neck.

He answered by picking her up and carrying her back to the bedroom.

CHAPTER 17

They left Waite Inn with a reservation to celebrate their first anniversary next year. As Jonathan drove down the tree-lined lane, Carrie absentmindedly dragged her fingers across his thigh as she replayed some of the more memorable moments from the past few days. She felt like the luckiest woman on the planet—the happiest too.

They'd have one night at home all together before flying to Disneyland with the kids. She had a move-out inspection scheduled at her house in the evening, and then she could focus on their new life with Jonathan. With her mom's sudden illness, she had missed out on the chance to pack everything up in her little house and move it over to Jonathan's. But Jenny and Max had stepped in and taken care of everything. Already Carrie felt like part of an extended family, even though it was a small one.

"I guess everything went OK with the kids. Well, nothing catastrophic happened, or Lisa would've called."

"Do you think she'll ever find a partner?" Jonathan questioned. "She seems to always be taking care of everyone around here, and the kids were thrilled to have her watching them, but I often wonder if she's lonely."

"I'd love that for her, but she was really traumatized by her dad's coldness when she was growing up. It's like she refuses to even be open to the idea of a relationship. Honestly, it would take a miracle."

"Like us getting together? That sure felt like a miracle to me!"

She shifted to face him. "The best miracle," she agreed.

Lisa greeted them at the door. She was ready to head out, dressed in jeans, black ankle boots, and an indigo blue knitted sweater peeking out from a sheepskin coat.

"Welcome home you guys!" she hugged both of them and then stepped back to look at Carrie. Nodding almost to herself, she added, "I think this marriage thing will be alright for you."

Carrie felt herself blushing. "Thanks! How were the kids?"

"*So* fun! I mean, I'll probably sleep for a week now, but that was the best weekend I've had in a long time. Call me any time you want to get away and I'll gladly come back! Oh, and Jonathan?"

He looked up at her from the trunk of the car where he was grabbing their suitcases. "Yeah?"

"You did a perfect job on the renos! I had Mom over here yesterday for the day, and she had a great time. Everything worked perfectly, and she even took the lift up to the second floor and had a nap in the guest room by herself."

A look of relief washed over his face as he walked towards them. "You have no idea how glad I am to hear that. I had to figure out the last bits myself with Carrie away."

"You did good. Now I'm going to let you two get settled in. Bye!" With a wave, she grabbed her own suitcase and made her way to her car parked on the street.

Carrie and Jonathan exchanged smiles and stepped through the door into their home.

PART II

CHAPTER 18

"Hi Lisa!"

Lisa took a big breath and turned around. Today was the day. She *needed* to talk to Aaron. No matter what. The weekend with Jonathan and Carrie's kids convinced her of something she had vaguely known for months. She wanted more from life. A partner and a family. And she was looking right at the man who wouldn't leave her thoughts alone.

"Hey, how are you?" She wondered he could see how nervous she was.

"Good! Very good! Here, let me help you." He reached past her and took the three snow shovels, and a bucket of eco-friendly rock salt out of her trunk. It was probably overkill, but she wanted to make sure the tenants had what they needed when the snow came.

"Thanks!"

"Guess you're all set for the snow then," he said as they walked towards the tool shed at the back of the property. Lisa was responsible for managing the building that she and her friends had invested in five months ago. It provided accessible, affordable housing and was the biggest and most fulfilling project Lisa had ever participated in.

Aaron lived next door and seemed to always be available to help. He had become a good friend, but Lisa was long past thinking of him as just a friend. After unlocking the shed and carefully storing the supplies, Lisa locked it up and turned to Aaron.

He stood a good five inches taller than Lisa, with short black hair, perfect dark skin, and glasses in front of dark brown eyes that were perpetually crinkled at the corners from laughing. Aaron had a laugh that was like water dancing over rocks on a mountain stream — delightful and soothing all at once.

Lisa refused to let her vision travel down his body, but this single dad of two stayed in very good shape. She didn't know how he managed it, because he was always offering her baking or inviting her over for a mouth-watering meal.

"Um, where are the kids?"

"Liam's gone to convince Cherish to get some bike riding in before the snow comes. And Thea's still at daycare."

"Oh, ok. Um…" Lisa was never afraid to speak her mind. Except today. Today she could feel herself shaking inside. She needed to tell him about her feelings for him. There was a tiny chance he felt the same way. After all, they spent time together every week. And she often accepted his invitation to come in for a drink or a meal. But even if he felt the same way, would he even want to do anything about it?

His ex-wife left when Aaron refused to 'fix' the kids. With a transgender son and an autistic daughter, they weren't exactly a typical family. But Lisa loved both kids exactly the way they were, even though it had taken months for Thea to accept her as one of the safe adults in her life.

She knew Aaron's entire focus was on his kids. He lived for them, and he was the best dad she had ever met. Maybe that's all he

wanted in life. Not to mention Lisa was white. Adding a biracial relationship into the mix might be too much—even for someone as big-
hearted as Aaron.

He put his arm gently on Lisa's arm, and she felt heat flow all the
way through her body. "Hey, is everything OK?"

She took a big breath, "Do you... um, can we walk?"

"Of course!"

They fell into step naturally and Lisa tried to organize her thoughts.
Aaron seemed in no rush to make her speak. The air had that crisp
feeling to it that came before the first snow of the year. Lisa was glad
for the way it hit her burning cheeks. She tried to breathe deep and
calm her pounding heart.

"So, here's the thing..." She looked up at him. No matter what he
said, she'd never stop loving him. He was everything she didn't even
know she wanted until they met. "I don't know how you'll feel about
this. I mean, it's really unexpected and I've never imagined this could
happen to me. Trust me on that. Um, the thing is... I've got feelings
for you. Strong feelings. I'm so sorry. It's not what I planned at all.
But I had to tell you."

Aaron slowed, then stopped. Lisa turned and looked up at him. At
least she knew he'd be kind about it. He didn't have a mean bone in
his body. They stood there, frozen in a moment full of questions and
surprises.

He opened his mouth, closed it, and then opened it again. "Lisa. I
don't know what to say—"

"—you don't need to say anything. Honest." She tried to read his
face, to figure out what he was thinking, but she couldn't.

"Well, I'd better head back. To pick up Thea..." his voice trailed off.

Lisa felt her heart sink. The last thing she wanted was to create an
awkwardness between them. "Of course!" she added brightly. "I'll
walk back with you. I wanted to say a quick hello to Mr. Martin

anyway. Did you know that he's mentoring a lady Carrie knows from the women's center? She's always wanted to be an electrician of all things and now he's going to help her get through her schooling." She kept a steady stream of conversation going until they were in front of the walkway to the housing complex.

"Well, uh, have a good evening then. Hopefully Thea had a good day! Bye!" She quickly turned before she could make eye contact. His soft goodbye was almost too quiet for her to hear.

Ignoring the landscaping and little playground that always gave her so much joy to see, she walked around to the back of the building and the entry to Mr. Martin's place. As soon as she rang the doorbell, she heard him holler to come up. Letting herself in she climbed the stairs to his suite while giving herself firm instructions to ignore whatever was going on in her heart.

"There's my favorite bookkeeper! Come on in and help me eat the cinnamon buns that Aaron dropped off yesterday. I swear, that man's gonna give me diabetes with all the food he brings by!"

Lisa left her shoes at the top of the stairs and hung her jacket over a chair in the tiny eating nook. She loved the efficient way the suite was laid out, with just enough space for one person, and maybe a visitor for tea and dessert once in a while.

"Have you seen our favorite neighbor already this afternoon?" he asked while bringing over a plate with a cinnamon bun on it.

"Uh, yeah. He helped me bring over the snow shovels and salt for the pathways. It's all in the shed now, but make sure you leave the shoveling to the younger people OK?" Lisa felt an almost motherly sense of concern for the tenants in the complex. Each one of them had arrived with their own challenges and heartbreak, but together they made a strong little community.

Below Mr. Martin lived Nicole, who had been evicted from her old apartment in a disturbing case of disability discrimination. Lisa was delighted to have been able to offer her one of their fully accessible suites, and now Nicole worked as the shipping manager for the clothing business that Lisa's friend Jaz operated.

Beside Nicole lived 13-year-old Cherish and her mom Nancy. They had been tenants of the building in the past before being pushed out by increasing rents, and were happy to be back in their own neighborhood and the freshly-renovated, affordable suite. Nancy worked as a care aide and she kept an eye on Nicole and Mr. Martin in between shifts. Cherish was best friends with Aaron's son Liam, and the two of them were practically inseparable.

"The city actually sent out a brochure saying how dangerous it is for us old people to try to shovel snow in the mornings," Mr. Martin chuckled. "Nice of them to be so concerned! But I'm quite happy to sit out the bad weather when it comes. Did I ever tell you about the job I had wiring a new apartment building in the dead of winter...?" He launched into one of his stories about working as an electrician, and Lisa was happy for the distraction from her own thoughts.

Driving home an hour later, Lisa tried to give herself a pep talk. *You've been perfectly fine with the single life up until now. Nothing's changed. And once the awkwardness of your confession to Aaron wears off, you can go back to being friends with him again. Come on, Lisa! You've got a great job doing freelance bookkeeping, being the finance officer for the Jazzy Clothing Company is a dream come true, and you'll be just fine. Plus, the last thing your mom needs right now is anything to worry about. A little bit of a broken heart is nothing compared to what she's been through!*

By the time she got home she almost believed herself. Alex's screams of delight when she walked in the door made her smile. His army-crawl style of transportation was becoming more efficient every day, and he made it to the front door by the time she had her shoes and coat off.

"Hello mister!" she said as she picked him up. He tolerated a quick cuddle before wiggling furiously to be let down. Lisa set him down gently and laughed as he crawled away into the living room. She followed him and found her mom sitting with her feet up in her recliner. It was Lisa's first Christmas gift to her mom the year that they reunited, and it allowed Maria to stand up with the help of the motorized seat. Beside it sat Maria's wheelchair, a constant reminder that her rheumatoid arthritis dictated her day's productivity.

"Well? Is the complex ready for winter?" she asked.

Lisa sat down on the couch beside her. "Yep! We should be good now. And I've added a note for next October to be ready earlier. We're lucky the harsh weather has held off." She looked up at the sound of Jaz hopping over the baby gate installed at the stairs.

"Oh my gosh! Whatever you have in the crock pot smells amazing! When's supper?" Jaz bounced into the room wearing one of her signature black and white outfits and sat down on the floor. Alex immediately made a beeline to his mom and crawled over her legs. "Hey you! I thought that baby gym class would wear you out!" She held him up and he started jumping up and down.

Lisa tried to relax into the very untraditional family unit that made up her life. Her mom would be 50 in a few years—she had the spirit of a teenager, but the physical challenges of someone much older thanks to the harsh effects of rheumatoid arthritis on her body. Jaz had just turned 20, and Alex would be one year old in February. At 25, Lisa sometimes felt like she was the man in the family. Sure, she loved dressing up, getting her hair done, and having girls' nights out. But she was also the one who maintained the house and the car, protected her mom, Jaz, and Alex, and supported the family on her earnings.

Working for the Jazzy Clothing Company took up most of her time during the week. Jaz still ran a division that upcycled used clothing bought at thrift stores and online auctions, and provided at-home work for her team of seamstresses. But her new venture into producing stylish, accessible clothing was becoming a massive undertaking. Even with the guidance of Jaz's dad, who acted as unofficial vice-president of the company, dealing with suppliers, overseas factories, and all the financial logistics of launching a line of clothing kept Lisa happily busy.

Giving her head a shake, she forced herself to pay attention to the here and now—something Carrie was always saying. Standing up, she made her way into the kitchen to finish making supper. Thanks to Aaron's advice, she often prepped a variety of meals that could go from freezer to crock pot in the morning and be ready at supper time without much added effort. Just another way he made her life nicer.

Tonight they were eating Moroccan Chicken Stew and the aroma of paprika, turmeric, and ginger was making her mouth water. She put a pot on to boil for rice and then started to set the table.

Jaz joined her. "I wonder if Alex will like this one as much as the creamy chicken you made last week! We're so lucky you make food he can eat too. I was reading on one of those Mommy blogs about how you shouldn't give your baby that canned baby food."

Lisa looked at Jaz and rolled her eyes. "Have you found any blogs that just tell moms to do what they think is best for their kids?"

"Not everyone's a free spirit like you, Lisa. Some of us *want* to be told what to do!"

"Well, I'm pretty sure you're doing a great job with Alex. What was it like at the baby gym?" Lisa went with Jaz the first time she took him to the activity class. She had never felt so scrutinized in all her life. But for Jaz's sake, she forced herself to chat with the other moms and try to make friends. They had both been pleasantly surprised. It's as if the whole world was full of women trying desperately to get everything right.

She had always been happy—proud even—to be a supportive friend to Jaz. Why did she suddenly wish she was a mom too? And now that Aaron was scared off, what should she do? She knew she wanted a life with him, Liam, and Thea. If she couldn't have that, did she still want family life but with someone else? And *why* couldn't she just be content with her life right now?

"Halloooo! Earth to Lisa!"

She looked down at the plates in her hand and wondered how long she had been standing there. Seriously. What was her problem?

"Oh!" She let out a short laugh. "Um, sorry. Got lost in the clouds there for a moment!" She quickly set the table and then turned to the rice cooking while avoiding looking directly at Jaz. Out of the corner of her eye she saw her pause for a moment, and then turn to the crock pot to puree some food for Alex.

CHAPTER 19

Lisa woke up the next morning determined to put her crush on Aaron behind her and focus on the reality of her life. She had a few hours to deal with bookkeeping for her freelance clients before driving her mom to physiotherapy. Then, in the afternoon there was a Jazzy Clothing Company meeting at their house with Jaz's dad and George Chen. Mr. Chen was an old friend of Jaz's dad and had extensive international business experience. The two men offered Jaz their help in a bit of a patronizing way to start, but now they were solidly behind both her expansion plans and her ability to quickly grow a successful business.

Every time Mr. Chen came over, Lisa wondered if he'd put two and two together and realize that Jaz's son had more than passing resemblance to his own son, Ellison. A one night stand in high school left Jaz pregnant and Ellison desperate that nobody would know of his involvement. Jaz nearly kept her word, and only her closest friends knew the identity of Alex's father.

As Lisa enjoyed her coffee, she listened for sounds of her mom getting up. Mornings were often difficult for Maria, and sometimes she asked Lisa for a little help getting dressed. It was like a knife to her heart to see her mom in pain and struggling to complete even the simplest of daily tasks.

No matter how much money Lisa made, or how carefully she took care of her mom, there was no way to go back in time and get her the care she needed when she first received the arthritis diagnosis. At the time, Lisa's dad still controlled every aspect of his wife's life, and he didn't think Maria needed treatment, medication, or doctor's visits. He was dead now, but the damage done to Maria's body was irreversible.

Hearing the 'oof' that indicated her mom was settled in her wheelchair, Lisa got up to make her tea. She didn't know if anything they were doing now helped, but that wouldn't stop her from trying. The smell of green tea mingled with Lisa's coffee. It was a comforting reminder of a routine they both enjoyed.

"Morning dear!" Maria said cheerfully as she slowly wheeled herself over to the table.

"Morning Mom," Lisa answered, leaning over to kiss her on the cheek while placing a mug with a plastic straw in it in front of her. Maria looked up with a twinkle in her eye.

"Don't even start!" Lisa warned. "I will not have you impaling yourself on a metal straw. We are doing *a lot* to reduce our waste and energy usage. A couple of straws a day is a 'sacrifice' I'm willing to make in exchange for you being able to drink comfortably and not die."

"Speaking of that, I booked the electrician to come out next Tuesday to install the car charger. And I think having that as an amenity will be nice for our Airbnb guests, too."

"I still can't believe I bought a new car. I mean, who does that? Just goes out and buys a brand new car?" Lisa shook her head in disbelief.

"Probably the same type of person who buys a house at 23, takes care of her mom, and helps run an international clothing company."

The pride in Maria's voice was unmistakable. They had worked hard to build a relationship after her dad died, and Lisa still felt a little boost to know her Mom was proud of her.

"How *are* you doing with everything?"

Lisa looked up at her mom. She hadn't told anyone about her feelings for Aaron. The only person who knew was Mr. Martin, and it still frustrated her that her feelings were so clearly obvious on the day he called her on it. After years of having no interest in guys or dating, she still felt overwhelmed and conflicted about Aaron. She wondered if her face somehow gave her secret away.

"Well…" she wracked her brain for something to tell her mom, "I'm thinking of looking for more property!" There! That should explain any weirdness that her mom and Jaz might have picked up on.

"Ohhhh, Lisa! That's so exciting! What do you have in mind?"

Lisa looked at her mom. What had she just done? Had she really lied to her mom, just because she was trying to ignore her feelings for Aaron?

The ping of her phone rescued her. "Oh, that's my new client with the files I need to get started."

"Go ahead and get to work. We can chat while you drive me to physio later."

Lisa tried to ignore a guilty nudge as she got laptops and a file folder out of the buffet they used for office storage in the dining room. She set up her mom's laptop first and then did what she always did when she was feeling upset—bury herself in work.

When Jaz came downstairs with Alex, Lisa had almost forgotten her earlier lie, and Jaz set Alex in her lap while she went to get his breakfast ready. Mornings were one of the only times he was calm enough to sit still for cuddles.

He had that delicious baby smell that she was beginning to long for, and when he laid his head on her shoulder, she felt something inside of her crave a child of her own. *Seriously Lisa, get a stinkin' grip! Alex is all you need—and you don't have to get up at night with him! Be grateful for what you have!*

"Lisa? You have the weirdest look on your face. Are you… are you crying?" Jaz quickly sat down beside her and grabbed her hand. "What's wrong?"

Maria looked up, concern immediately crossing her face.

"Um, oh. You know, I think I have allergies or something. Maybe I need to see the doctor."

"Allergies? In November? Is that a thing?"

"I really don't know!" It was the first honest thing she said all morning. She quickly wiped her eyes and dropped her gaze down to Alex so her mom and her best friend wouldn't see her face. *That was weird,* she thought. It wasn't like her to be emotional. Maybe she needed to schedule a session with Carrie when she got back from Disneyland.

"Hey!" Her voice sounded unusually loud. "Has anyone heard from Carrie?"

"Yep! Check Facebook. She posted a bunch of adorable pictures last night. I can't wait to take Alex there!"

Lisa reached up with one hand to open a Facebook tab on her laptop and Alex immediately tried to grab the keys. She pushed the laptop out of reach. "Alright buddy. You get my full attention until Mommy has your breakfast ready."

"Put him in his highchair and I'll give him some Cheerios. He'll be fine!"

Lisa reluctantly buckled him into his highchair. He didn't mind, but she would have rather kept holding him. Sitting back down she read through Carrie's post and looked at the pictures. "Oh my gosh! Did you see the one of Katie and the Disney princesses? She actually looks speechless!"

"I'm there right now! I hope they videotaped that!"

Lisa watched her mom's face as she scrolled through the post. The new computer mouse she'd found seemed to be easier for her to use, but it looked big and clunky. At least there were some products that made life a little easier. Her mom was also learning to use dictation to handle more tasks, so she didn't have to type as much. *What do people do who don't have money for all these accessibility add-ons? I wonder if there's a foundation or something to help with that...*

"Lisa?"

"Huh? Oh, sorry. Lost in thought again."

"Do you need a vacation or something? You keep spacing out lately. I thought that was my job!" Jaz teased.

Lisa smiled, "You can't have all the spacey fun! I was just watching Mom with her new mouse and wondering what disabled people who can't afford things that would make their life easier do. I mean, that mouse, plus using Google Home has really made things easier. But getting it all and setting it up isn't cheap."

"Ooohh, we have to be able to do something about that!" Jaz's experiences since getting pregnant exposed her to a different world than the privileged one in which she grew up. Her awareness of social problems related to money and her rapidly growing bank account meant she was always on the lookout for ways to help others. It had been her idea to buy a building exclusively to rent out as affordable housing, and her relentless optimism for big projects kept Lisa and Maria sprinting to keep up.

"Well, Christmas is coming. Do you think we could do one of those adopt-a-family things, but ask specifically for one with a disabled family member?"

"Mom, that's brilliant! We could give them a whole wardrobe from Jaz's clothing line and find products that make their life easier! Maybe we could even pay for some renovations if their house isn't that good for them!"

"Ah, there's the light back in your eyes! I'm glad to see it. I'll do some research while I'm resting this afternoon and see what I can find. Now, are we ready for our meeting this morning?"

Lisa mentally shifted gears to the Jazzy Clothing Company. "Yep. I'm sure both of them have checked over the new balance sheets I finished yesterday."

"And I have my list of things to do all ready," Jaz added as she walked over to the table with Alex's breakfast. "The only unknown is whether or not Alex will go down for his nap. It was a lot easier when we met on Saturdays and Mom could watch him."

"I know! But, ironically enough, your dad doesn't have Saturdays free anymore since retiring!"

Jaz rolled her eyes. "Him and golf."

"He sure is happier than when we first met him! I'm glad he's taking his health seriously and enjoying his weekends. I wonder how he'll feel about golfing after having Alex for the night?"

Jaz's parents had recently baby-proofed the house and converted Jaz's old bedroom into a nursery for Alex. This Friday would be his first 'sleepover' at ma-ma and pa-pa's, and then her parents would drop him off Saturday morning on the way to the golf course.

"Depends on how he does at night, I guess. And I'm already kinda freaking out about *not* having him here for the night!"

"We'll do our best to keep your mind busy!" Maria promised. She had splurged on tickets to Cirque du Soleil for the three of them, and they were rounding out the night with dinner out before the show. Although Maria usually encouraged Jaz and Lisa to get out and 'be young', this was one outing where she decisively included herself.

"You two will love it!" Jaz gushed. "I still have such amazing memories of going when I was 12. I tried to get my mom and dad to buy tickets this time too, but they figured it wouldn't be any different. Their loss!"

"And your gain, since you get a babysitter out of it!"

"Well, there is that!" Just as she scraped the last of Alex's baby cereal onto her spoon, he let out a huge sneeze that sprayed her, the highchair, and even the floor. She sat there in shock for a moment before they all burst out laughing. Alex gave his head a little shake as if to clear the food from his face and then joined them.

"I think we need to make a recording of his laughs and just give them away to sad people!" Maria said, wiping her eyes. "Even if whatever happened wasn't funny—and this was—his baby laugh just makes my day!"

Lisa helped Jaz clean up the mess before they all went their own ways for an hour. She made herself focus on her freelance work and managed to stop her mind from wandering to Aaron for nearly the entire time.

CHAPTER 20

"OK, I don't know what it is about watching those performances, but I have a ton of new clothing ideas flying through my head now!"

They were on their way home after being transported to a different world for the last two hours. Maria asked Jaz about her ideas, but Lisa didn't say much.

It had been different for her. One row in front and a few seats over from her a young family sat with what looked like a nine-year-old and a six-year-old. While the show had been impressive, she kept being drawn back to the expressions of awe on the kids' faces, and the pleasure the parents clearly got out of their children's experience.

She knew the show probably wouldn't appeal to Thea, but she wished she would have bought a ticket for Liam and included him. Two hours of being transported to an otherworldly place would have been therapeutic for him. About a week before she had 'the talk' with Aaron, he told her that puberty was starting to change Liam's body in ways he was having a hard time coping with.

After her first meeting with him in the spring—when he stormed out of the house with fists on hips because she was talking to Thea—she naturally saw him as a boy, although his birth certificate said otherwise. He came across as a fiercely protective older brother, willing to do anything to protect his little sister. It *had* taken a few visits for him to realize Lisa was someone he could trust, but now they had a solid friendship.

Knowing he struggled with a body that didn't match who he was broke her heart. Even though he was confident and generally happy, she didn't want him to have to go through all the crap that normally went with being in high school on top of being transgender and 'different' than almost everyone else. A night out might have helped, even just for a little while.

And then she wondered about all the kids who would never see a show like the one that night. Those tickets were crazy expensive, and there was no way most families could afford it. But every child deserved to experience it, just like the two kids in front of her did.

Her mind wandered to Carrie, and her kids. At least now, with Carrie's successful business and Jonathan's support, they could do things like go to Disneyland.

"Have you ever been to Disneyland?" she blurted out to Jaz.

"What? Yeah, a couple of times. They have some pretty amazing shows there too, but nothing to the level that we saw tonight."

Lisa looked in the rearview mirror at her. Jaz had on a half-smile. Either from the night or her memories of Disneyland. "I can't wait to take Alex!" she said again through a yawn.

And there it was again. The chance to experience the world through a child's eyes. Was that what she needed? It didn't make sense. She always focused on goals she could achieve—by herself if necessary. Having children required a guy. And children. She shook her head. Nope. That probably wasn't going to happen.

She parked in the driveway and went around to get the wheelchair out of the trunk. Jaz had already opened Maria's car door and went to unlock the front door. Lisa carefully positioned the wheelchair and locked the wheels before wiggling in between the open door and the wheelchair.

"Can you help with the legs tonight?" her mom asked in a quiet voice.

Lisa hoped it was just the shadows from the front porch light that creased her mom's face in pain, but she knew better than that. They had enjoyed such a good night out, but it was late, and her mom didn't usually need to transfer from car to wheelchair multiple times in the evening. Now they'd pay the price.

She put one hand against the seat and lifted her mom's arm to rest on hers. Then with her other hand she gently reached under her mom's knees and carefully rotated her body until her feet were on the ground. Her mom blew out a breath in pain.

The next step was the one Lisa hated. She tucked her hands carefully behind her mom's elbows like the physiotherapist taught her and then looked in her mom's eyes. "Ready?" she asked.

Her mom nodded. "One, two, three," she whispered.

On 'three' Lisa pulled and her mom leaned forward until she was standing on her feet. Then they rotated just enough for Maria to drop into her wheelchair. Lisa reached to put the footrests down and lifted each of her mom's feet up and onto the metal plates.

"Thanks for the dance!" her mom said. She said it every time she needed Lisa to help her transfer to or from the wheelchair. It *was* a sort of dance, but one that broke Lisa's heart a little every time.

After grabbing both of their purses, closing up the car, and locking it, she pushed the wheelchair up the small ramp and into the house. Jaz had already gone into Maria's room to turn on the heating pad in her bed. She passed Maria and Lisa in the hallway and gave them each a hug goodnight before going upstairs.

Lisa carefully slipped off her mom's boots and wheeled her over to the rolling table beside the bed where Maria had laid out her night-time pills before they left. Her hands shook a little, and Lisa held the water bottle for her so she could take a drink.

"I'm pretty sure you'll need me for the whole routine tonight."

Maria nodded, and Lisa wheeled her into the bathroom. She parked beside the toilet and pulled her mom's nightgown off the hook on the back of the door. It wasn't often that she needed help to get undressed, thank goodness.

During times when her mom was sick with flares or the flu—things that happened at least a few times a year—Lisa hired a private nurse that took over all her mom's personal care. It was the least she could do to give her mom some dignity while her body slowly took it away.

This was different. By tomorrow or the next day Maria would be feeling better. And she could still use the toilet independently. But getting changed required quite the range of motion and grip strength —something her mom just didn't have tonight.

Lisa gently helped her mom get her top half undressed and slipped the nightgown on before they struggled together to deal with her bottom half. Once the nightgown was on and everything else was off Lisa helped her shuffle over to the toilet, and then left the room and closed the bathroom door behind her.

She busied herself with pulling out the heating pad now that the chill was out of the bed and turning down the covers until she heard her mom called quietly to her. Back in the bathroom she helped her finish getting ready for bed, and then wheeled her into her bedroom where they did their transfer dance one more time to get Maria into bed. Lisa made sure she had everything she needed within reach before kissing her mom goodnight and slipping out.

She walked to the kitchen and poured herself a glass of wine. A few minutes later, Jaz came downstairs in her pajamas, made a mug of hot chocolate, and sat down quietly beside her. Neither of them said anything. It wasn't necessary. They both knew that sometimes good days would follow bad days, sometimes bad days would follow good days, and Maria would continue to lose mobility and gain pain.

Lisa slowly sipped her wine and wished she had something strong enough to numb her own sadness. She tried to focus her thoughts on all the things she should be thankful for. Definitely having Jaz here helped. She never felt alone. But Jaz was moving with Alex to the basement suite soon. Even though they'd still technically be under the same roof, it wouldn't be the same. Lisa didn't even have the heart to list Jaz's room on Airbnb and take advantage of a chance to earn some extra income.

Her friendship with Carrie, Jonathan, and their kids was something to be thankful for. And the housing project that provided safe beautiful homes for four people who became good friends. Plus, there was the unique connection she had with Mr. Martin that filled a bit of the void in her life left by her cruel and cold father. Another good thing.

She took a big breath and let it out slowly. Tomorrow was Friday—a favorite day for all the women in the house—the day that Jaz's seamstresses brought in their completed projects, got paid, and received their 'assignments' for the following week. The house would be full of people coming and going in the morning, plus lots of laughter and chatter. Lisa hoped her mom would be up to joining them at the dining room table that also functioned as the base for their operations during the day. But if she couldn't, a few of the women would be sure to visit her in her bedroom. That was the best they could do.

Lisa got up, gave Jaz a shoulder hug, and rinsed out her glass before making her way upstairs. She felt tired. Hopefully, enough for her to fall asleep and not be plagued by questions she didn't have answers to.

CHAPTER 21

The morning came quickly. Lisa forced herself out of bed as soon as her alarm went off and made her way downstairs to her mom's room. It was a good thing she had set it. Her mom needed to get to the bathroom and couldn't wait for her pain pills to kick in. Lisa helped her get up, into the wheelchair, to the bathroom, onto the toilet, back in the wheelchair, and back to bed. She helped her take her pills and then went around and climbed into the bed on the other side.

As a little girl, she was never allowed in her parent's bed—another one of her dad's rules. Now climbing into bed beside her mom was an act of defiance against his memory. She rolled over and watched her mom's eyelids flutter closed. Soon her even breathing told Lisa she was OK, and she allowed herself to fall back asleep too.

She woke up to the sound of someone knocking on the front door. It took a minute to remember that Jaz's parents were dropping off Alex early before going golfing. She listened to the quiet hum of voices interspersed with Alex squealing and chattering away. As soon as the door closed, she got up and went to see them.

"There's the man of the house!" she smiled at Alex but didn't even offer to take him. It was clear by the way Jaz held him tight that she had missed him and he had missed her.

"Did everything go OK?" she asked Jaz.

"Yep! They think he's ready to spend a weekend with him, especially since it will probably be too cold to golf on Saturdays for a while…" her voice faded off and she swallowed hard. "I'm probably being silly about the whole thing—never thought I'd be a clingy mom. I can't believe how much he's a part of me now!"

Lisa ruffled Alex's hair and went to make coffee for herself and tea for her mom and Jaz. Hopefully, her mom could relax in bed and drink her tea before needing to go to the bathroom again.

Three hours later the house was full of the sound of women chatting. Lisa paused after writing a check to one seamstress so she could watch her mom. Maria insisted on getting dressed and being at the table before everyone came. Lisa suspected being around people and activity helped her mom ignore her pain. But she still looked worn out. Chances are, she'd spend the rest of the day in bed.

Having a quiet house wasn't good for Lisa either. As soon as the busyness of the morning passed, she felt like she had too much time to think about Aaron. It was ridiculous really. She had operated with laser sharp focus from the minute she left home on the day of her high school graduation. She had worked two jobs, put herself through night school, worked up the corporate ladder, bought a house, started her own bookkeeping business, and helped Jaz grow her empire. All without being distracted. There was no reason to change now, but her thoughts and feelings seemed out of her control.

Somehow by suppertime she had completed all her freelance work for the week and confirmed the Jazzy Clothing Company's books were up to date. That was a job she could almost always work on, since orders came in online at all times of the day and night. But she had a good system set up that allowed her to keep an almost-constant eye on the situation when needed.

In some ways, Jaz had moved her focus from affordable housing to designing accessible clothing, but Lisa was OK with that. She liked being the one to oversee the project on a long-term basis. She was still looking for the right people to occupy three of the units in the complex. In the meantime, two of them were listed with Airbnb which kept Lisa busy.

Her friend Carla, who used to live in the basement suite, used to do all the cleaning for the Airbnb units. But now Chris and Carla were happily living in their newly renovated dream home and operating a successful construction company. They still came with their daughter Becky to visit at least a few times a month, but Carla had her hands full with the company and couldn't keep cleaning for Lisa.

There were a few weeks when she did all the cleaning herself and she scolded herself about her lack of physical fitness. It was hard to even remember being tough enough to clean an entire office building after a waitressing shift. She wondered if she should sign up for an exercise class or something!

Her latest cleaner was a guy that came highly recommended by Nancy who met him through a client. Lisa had a moment of thinking a guy probably couldn't do a good job cleaning before coming to her senses and deciding to give him a try. In his second week of working for her, she was impressed.

Calvin didn't talk about himself much, and she got the impression he had a rough past. But he was determined to do a good job for Lisa. They'd agreed that he would text her when he finished cleaning up after the weekend guests and she'd double check his work. If he did a good job, then she'd leave him to it, and only check occasionally.

But what she really wanted was to get deserving families into the final three suites. Once Carrie was back from Disneyland, she'd ask for her help.

Saturday Jaz woke up with a terrible cold. It was crazy how quick a cough seemed to take hold. She and Jaz agreed that Jaz would stick to her room and Lisa would watch Alex and limit contact with Jaz. If they were lucky, the virus would leave Maria alone.

Although Lisa hated knowing her friend felt so terrible, she loved spending the day with Alex. He asked for 'mama' throughout the day, but she could easily distract him. After his morning nap, Lisa bundled him up and took him out for a walk. The forecast called for snow that night so she figured they'd better get their fresh air while they could.

Without really thinking about it she walked past Jaz's parents' house. They were just pulling into the driveway and invited Lisa and Alex in.

Immediately Jaz's mom went into over-parenting mode. "Here," she said placing a packed grocery bag in the bottom of the stroller, "I have put a bag of oranges, some fresh ginger, and some good echinacea tea in there. You make sure she takes it all. She is too thin to be sick!"

Lisa relaxed on the white couch in their elegant living room while Jaz's dad sat on the floor and played with Alex. "It looks like having a grandson has interrupted your color scheme!" she commented. The only colorful things in the room were Alex's toys. It looked like they had doubled the collection since Lisa had last been there.

He smiled at Alex before looking up, "I think it's a wonderful addition. Very stylish."

"Well," said Jaz's mom as she brought a cup of tea for Lisa and then sat primly on the edge of the white Sloan armchair, "black and white toys are not appropriate for this age. He needs his senses stimulated."

She looked at Lisa thoughtfully. "I think you should talk to Jaz about getting him into the Mandarin school. If she does not start the process soon, he will miss out."

Lisa held up her free hand, "I'm just the babysitter here! No advice from me, except to tell her to keep doing what she's doing. I don't know how she figures out all the parenting while dealing with so much for the business."

"It seems to come naturally to her," Jaz's dad agreed. "What about you? When will you have a family?"

Lisa took a second to remind herself that Jaz's parents meant well, even if they were a bit pushy. "Well, it's not something I wanted until recently. But it's also not really something I have any control over!"

"If you were Chinese, your mom could find you a nice man!"

Lisa laughed out loud, "If I was Chinese I would stay at home all day and eat my mom's cooking!"

Deciding it was time to deflect any further pressure about her future, she asked about their most recent golf game, and spent the next half an hour listening to the two of them talk about their favorite sport. She knew their story—how Jaz's dad got another girl pregnant who refused to keep the baby, and Jaz's mom offered to marry him and help raise Jaz. Their marriage had started out as an agreement of convenience and nothing more, but they were clearly soulmates now who loved each other deeply. *That's* what she wanted.

CHAPTER 22

The snow started falling on Sunday and didn't let up. Lisa reveled in the chance to get outside and shovel snow every couple of hours. The snow was wet and heavy, and the effort needed to keep the sidewalk and driveway clear somehow helped her feel a little less morose about her own situation.

Normally she and Aaron texted throughout the week, and he invited her for at least dessert if not a meal. The total silence from him upset her, even though she figured it was her fault for exposing her heart to him like that.

Maria had recovered from their late night outing, and the two of them worked hard to keep Alex occupied while his mom tried to recover from her cold. They also decided Lisa would take her into the clinic in the morning if her cough didn't improve. When Alex went down for his afternoon nap, Lisa collapsed on the sofa and looked at her mom.

"Was it this... intense when I was a baby?"

"Oh no, not at all! Actually, sometimes I worried you'd never walk! You were so happy to just sit there and play with whatever toys you could reach. I could be in the kitchen for half an hour and I'd come back to the living room, and you'd be in the same place! When you did decide to walk the only thing that changed is you'd walk to wherever I was with a toy in each hand and plop down beside me to play." She looked at Lisa thoughtfully. "I never would have guessed you'd grow up to be so ambitious and driven."

"Well, at first I was just desperate to make it on my own so I wouldn't have any reason to see Dad again... but then after a while I think I got hooked on the feeling of accomplishment. High school was so hard. Well, except for accounting class. I never really felt like I succeeded. I just barely passed. So the first time I got an A in college it was pretty amazing."

A look of regret passed over Maria's face. "I wish I could have been there to celebrate with you."

"Me too Mom. But I think Dad would have done everything he could to minimize it and put me down." She smiled, but felt sad, "It's a lot easier to do well when no one's trying to bring you down."

"It's hard. Even after talking with Carrie, and everything she said about how I need to forgive myself and focus on today and tomorrow. It's hard to know I just let him treat you so badly."

"Carrie's right Mom. You were doing everything you could to survive. I still can't believe he threatened to take me away from you. He was a horrible man, but he's gone now and we have done pretty darn good since!"

"We sure have!" She smiled through a yawn. "I'm going to get some rest while our little tiger is sleeping."

Lisa waited until her mom transferred from her recliner to her wheelchair and then got up and gave her a hug. Even though she started her adult life completely alone, she wasn't alone now and that was worth everything.

On a whim, she texted Aaron:

Hey, I hope that what I said last week doesn't impact our friendship. It might feel weird for a bit, but I want to get past that and stay friends.

Almost immediately she got a reply back:

lisa? it's liam. dad lent me his phone cause I forgot mine at a friends. i'll pass ur msg when i'm back home

Lisa was horrified. At least she hadn't said anything more in her text, but still. It never occurred to her that someone other than Aaron might read his texts! She put her face in her hands and rubbed hard for a moment. Well, it was done now, so she texted back.

Oh, hey you! How's it going? I guess the snow's put a stop to your biking.

yeah. it sucks. had to take the bus and it was freezing waiting.

Well, if you need a ride home or anything just text me, k?

k. thx.

She hadn't expected Aaron to be at home in the middle of the day. That meant Thea was having a rough day. When that happened, Lisa knew that Aaron would do his best to stay at home and put as few demands as possible on her. Autism with Thea meant always being flexible. Aaron did really well at figuring out what triggered her, but sometimes there was no way of knowing what she was experiencing or why it was so overwhelming.

Lisa had spent enough time with the family to recognize when Thea was experiencing sensory overload, but not enough time to understand what was causing it. One time Aaron knew right away it was the neighbor across the street using a leaf blower and he quickly got Thea's noise canceling headphones on her. Lisa hadn't even noticed the sound. It would be easier if Thea could tell them what bothered her, but all she could manage was signing 'no' over and over while they tried to figure out what to stop.

When that didn't work, Aaron would try to get her into the sensory room he built for her in the basement. It included all kinds of things that she could use to calm herself down—toys she liked to touch, a chair she could spin in circles, and lights that she could control. It also meant that he'd be housebound until she calmed down.

At least Liam could bike during the summer and take the bus in the winter. He was the opposite of his little sister. Always seeking out something new to do or see. He would have loved to be in sports, but at twelve years old all the organized sports segregated boys and girls. Even if he was accepted on a boys' team, Aaron felt there were too many chances for problems in change rooms or even on the field. So Liam kept himself busy without being on a team.

As Lisa sat and thought about him and his situation an idea started to grow. He needed something physical and challenging to do. And she needed to find some activity to get back in shape—but she didn't want to go to anything alone. Was there something she could do with Liam?

She grabbed her laptop and started typing. Rock climbing? Just the thought of it made her feet go cold. Yoga? Probably not something he'd want to try. Swimming? Nope, that probably required tricky change room decisions for Liam. Squash? Immediately Lisa visualized her and Liam running around a court dripping with sweat and wearing circa-1980s headbands. Must be something she remembered from a movie. But… it might be fun.

She'd have to talk to Aaron first, though. Maybe he didn't want her hanging out with his kids anymore. With a sigh, she closed her laptop. *Why* did she have to tell him she liked him? Why couldn't she be content with the way things were?

The sound of Alex calling out broke into her thoughts. She quickly went upstairs and was greeted with a smell that nearly made her gag.

"Seriously buddy? You couldn't have saved that for when Mommy's better?"

He squealed in excitement at seeing her and tried to jump up and down while holding onto the bars of the crib. Lisa couldn't help but smile. Maybe if she got good enough at squash, she could play it with Alex when he got bigger. But in the meantime, she had to get him cleaned up. She wished she could open the window a crack for some fresh air, but snow was blowing against it.

CHAPTER 23

Monday morning dawned bright and crisp. The snow stopped falling sometime during the night, and now the sun seemed to sparkle off every surface. Lisa took a moment to be grateful she didn't have to commute into downtown anymore. She imagined the roads didn't look quite as magical as her backyard did!

When Jaz came downstairs for breakfast she looked much better. "Maybe that tea from my mom really helped!" she said as she shifted Alex to her other hip and made his breakfast. He hung onto her tightly after a weekend with little contact.

"Well, I think you did a marvelous job of keeping your cold to yourself!" Maria smiled.

"I've got a ton of stuff to catch up on now though."

"You must have been going crazy! I don't think I've ever seen you not doing anything. I was so busy with Alex I didn't even think of you being bored." Lisa couldn't imagine a whole weekend where she couldn't get anything done.

"Actually, it was kinda good. I just lay in bed and listened to podcasts. There's a lot of stuff out there that's super helpful! And stories from other women who have built their own businesses from scratch. It made me wish that one day I could be the person giving the talk that inspires others." She came to the table balancing a bowl of baby food for Alex and a spoon in one hand, and Alex in the other.

"Seriously? You'd *want* to stand up in front of total strangers and talk?" That was the opposite of Lisa's dreams for her future.

"Um, yeah. Now that I get to spend every day designing clothes that make me happy, I think I just feel like I could do anything."

Maria took a slow sip of her tea. "Good for you! You're proving that it's fine to just go for what you want, no matter what your age is. I read all these books about women finding themselves after they retire. Which is good, but why not do it right away? Well, both of you girls have done that, haven't you?"

Lisa didn't answer. She had found herself for a while, but now it felt like she had lost herself again. What she needed was a heart to heart talk with Carrie. She finished her coffee and sent Carrie a text before going to make breakfast for the three of them:

> *Hey! Welcome back! I saw all of your posts from Disneyland. You look so cute together! When you've settled back in can we get together for a chat? I need some Carrie-wisdom in my life.*

By the time they were eating the omelets Lisa made, Carrie responded:

> *Hey back! I think I'm still floating on magic dust. Disneyland was sooooo much fun! And I have to do some errands this morning. Want to meet for lunch today? I'd love to chat!*

"I'm meeting Carrie for lunch today. Do you guys need me to pick anything up?"

Jaz looked up from trying to feed Alex a piece of her omelet. He clearly wasn't impressed with the texture and spit it back out. "How much stuff are you willing to get? I planned to go shopping on the weekend, so now I'm running low on almost everything."

"Give me a list. I can do it all after lunch no problem."

"We should have their whole family over for supper this weekend," Maria suggested. "Maybe we could have *everyone* over! I'll buy the food. We could invite Chris and Carla, and Aaron and the kids, and everyone from the complex, and Max and Jenny, and…" Her voice trailed off as she looked at Lisa and Jaz trying hard not to burst out laughing at her sudden excitement. "What? We haven't had everyone together since the summer! Well, except for Carrie's wedding I suppose. But that's not the same as us all relaxing together for hours. What do you think? Can I send out a big invite?"

"Of course, Mom." Lisa ignored the catch in her heart at the thought of seeing Aaron. She'd have to see him sometime, and it might be easier around a large group of people. "What do you want to serve for food?"

"We could get a big tray of lasagna from Luciano's, and Caesar salad and garlic bread from the grocery store. That way it's not much work. Oh, maybe you could cook up some plain noodles in case any kids don't like lasagna."

Lisa allowed herself to get swept up in her mom's excitement. She'd suffer through an awkward evening around Aaron to make her mom happy. And she'd get to see the kids. She cleaned up breakfast and got the table set up for a morning of work.

Two and a half hours later she closed her laptop with a satisfying click. She loved it when all the numbers lined up at the end of a task and she could send off a new, organized, and accurate file to her clients. Aaron felt the same way. As CFO of a large company he was equally enthusiastic about accounting and numbers. They would just be so good together! With a sigh, she got up to go see Carrie.

The roads were already well cleared, and she pulled up in front of the café with ten minutes to spare. She leaned back against the head-rest and closed her eyes. She had every intention of telling Carrie about Aaron. She needed her to know exactly what was going on, and hopefully she'd tell Lisa what to do. Although that wasn't Carrie's style. Lisa smiled to herself. Carrie had a knack for asking questions that forced you to figure things out for yourself.

A knock at her window caught her attention. She quickly grabbed her purse and got out of the car. Carrie looked amazing. Her brown hair had blonde highlights in it, her skin was glowing, and she had a huge smile.

"Wow! Disneyland looks good on you!" Lisa said as she reached out and hugged her friend.

"Thanks! It was awesome! And nice car!"

Lisa patted the roof of her car before walking with Carrie into the café. "Thanks! I'm officially gas-free and pollution-free. And it's *crazy* fun to be driving a brand new car!"

They went to the counter to order and then picked a cute round table set away in a corner.

"So," Carrie started, "tell me everything!"

Lisa raised an eyebrow, hesitated for a moment, and then dove in. "I totally need you to fix me. I can't even believe I'm saying this out loud but I've fallen in love, he's not interested, and I'm stuck on him."

Carrie's eyes got wide and her mouth dropped open. "What?"

She put her face in her hands. It was way worse to say it out loud. The soft touch of her friend's hand made her look up. Carrie's eyes were totally non-judgmental. But she still hadn't said anything.

"It gets worse," Lisa added. "It's Aaron."

"Aaron, the neighbor to our housing project?"

Lisa nodded, feeling miserable.

"Well. You've got excellent taste. That man is amazing. What happened?"

"We've been friends from almost the first time I saw the property. It's super easy to talk to him, and he's in finance so we have lots to talk about. And then Thea accepted me into her world and he started having me over for dinner or drinks once in a while. It was nothing. Until… until it was everything. I can't stop thinking about him, and Liam and Thea too."

She paused to let the server place their meals in front of them. Suddenly she didn't think she could eat the taco salad she'd ordered. "The weekend I watched Matthew and Katie was so much fun. I just loved being around them, and… I don't know… like I had a mission that made me feel really fulfilled. More than my work ever has. After that I asked Aaron if we could go for a walk and I told him I had feelings for him. He pretty much ended the conversation right there and I haven't heard from him since."

Carrie took a bite of her Rueben sandwich. She paused to chew, and Lisa wondered if she was stalling.

"I'm just trying to process what you're saying. And I think it must be doubly hard for you to process this. Am I right that this wasn't on your radar six months ago?"

"Yep. I thought the housing project, taking care of my mom and Jaz and Alex, and my work was enough. I was totally happy Carrie! Totally! And now I just feel terrible. The only person besides you who knows is Mr. Martin because he has this weird ability to see into my soul. Just by watching me talk to Aaron he knew how I felt! I thought it would go away. But now I want a family more than anything! And the guy I want it with isn't interested. What do I do?"

Carrie smiled. "In a big way, you can't do anything. However Aaron feels about you is out of your control. And he can't decide only based on his feelings. He's got the kids, and his world revolves around them."

"I know. But I want to be there for him and the kids. I love them too. Like crazy."

"Would you want to spend time with them even if Aaron didn't want a relationship?"

"Definitely. That's another thing I realized this week. I don't want my feelings for Aaron to get in the way of my relationship with them! I feel like I get Thea. And I'm not freaked out when she has a meltdown. I just want to make her world as safe as I can. And Liam is such a fantastic kid. I want to be there for him for the rest of his life. Like an aunty or something. But I have to figure out how to get past this thing for Aaron."

"OK... Tell me this. If you didn't have feelings for Aaron, but you still had all the knowledge about yourself that you've gained in the past while, what would you really, really want?"

Suddenly Lisa felt very interested in her taco salad. She took a few bites and was surprised to find it tasted really good. She thought about Carrie's question. No Aaron, but still feeling this way. That took a few minutes to work through.

"I guess... I think..." She took another bite and looked around the café. An elderly couple was sharing a sandwich. He carefully moved half onto his wife's plate and slid it over to her with an endearing smile. She didn't want that with anyone if it wasn't Aaron. And Carrie wanted her to answer as if there was no Aaron.

Beside the elderly couple sat a young woman with a little girl in a wheelchair. She was carefully feeding her one spoonful of soup at a time, carrying on what looked like a one-sided conversation. But then the girl looked right at the woman and Lisa could tell they had a real connection. The kind of connection she felt every once in a while with Thea.

"I want to help kids! I want to be a mom and have a connection with kids!" She slumped back in her chair. "Holy cow Carrie! I don't even know myself!"

"I disagree Lisa. Every choice you've made since you were fourteen and you mapped out a plan to succeed on your own was *because* you know yourself so well. Even this new revelation. You are constantly listening to your heart and doing what it tells you. What happened when you met Janet and found out that you could make a career out of working with numbers?"

Lisa thought back fondly to the moment when she had discovered her knack for numbers could turn into a job. "I enrolled in the book-keeping course."

"Exactly. And what happened when your dad died and your mom needed you?"

"I went and got her."

"Even though up until that moment you had no plans to take care of her."

Lisa nodded her agreement. It was obvious now what Carrie was getting at.

But she wasn't finished. "And what happened when you met a terri-fied, pregnant, nineteen-year-old?"

"I offered her a place to stay. OK, OK, I get it! And then when Jaz's company started to grow I took the leap and left my job so I could work for her and do freelancing. Which I still really enjoy, despite my current woes."

Carrie pointed a potato chip at her. "The thing is, every time you've faced something different from what you expected, you embraced it, and it made your life so much better! I can't make the heartache about Aaron go away. But I can promise that the pain eases over time. And maybe it's helped you see what's next for you. You know, you don't need a man to be a mom."

Lisa dropped her fork and it slipped off the table and onto the floor. "At least I wasn't taking a drink when you said that! What did you just say?"

"Lisa, there are a lot of ways to become a mom. You can adopt, you can become a foster mom, you can get in vitro fertilization. And honestly, there are probably a lot of great single dads out there looking for a life partner. But I don't think that last one's a good option unless you meet someone and have a connection with them outside of their kids."

The server came over and gave Lisa a clean fork. She smiled absently at her as she thanked her, and the fork dangled over her now-forgotten salad. Did she want kids in her life enough to do it on her own? For someone who had always seen herself living out her years with only her mom and her friends, it felt like too much to consider.

"Want to hear about Disneyland?"

Relief flooded over Lisa. "Yes please." Carrie seemed to completely understand what Lisa felt. She needed to step back from all the new thoughts for a moment and just let them sink in.

"So, before we were even in the main entrance Katie was practically exploding with excitement. Jonathan said she made the price of the tickets worth it in less than twenty seconds. Of course, everything was magical to her, and she totally flipped over every princess."

"Did she dress up?"

"Every day! And let me tell you, those dresses are a pain in the butt when a kid needs to go to the bathroom!"

Lisa found herself able to keep eating now. "What about Matthew?"

"He loved it almost as much as Katie. I can't even tell you what it felt like to see him totally relax and just be a carefree kid. Just...amazing."

"I'm so happy for you all! Oh, I almost forgot, Mom's planning a supper on Friday for pretty much everyone. She'll want to hear all about Disneyland! So, if you guys are free you can come and tell her everything."

"How's she doing?"

"Well, she's slowly getting worse, which we were warned would happen. But she hasn't had a flare in months. And she's still managing her personal care on her own for the most part. We went to see Cirque du Soleil last week, and she paid the price for that for a day and a half. But then she was back to her usual self. And what about your mom?"

"She's still got a cough, which is frustrating. But the infection's gone. She has an appointment with the specialist on Friday and then they're staying for the weekend—is it OK if we bring her and my dad to supper on Friday?"

"Are you kidding? Of course it's OK! Wow, even if you guys are the only ones who can make it, Mom will be delighted."

"I'm pushing for them to move here. You know, Mom never gets to visit friends where they live. Everyone has stairs. But here, she could even get an accessible taxi on her own if she wanted. And there's us, and you to visit, and so many more places here that are accessible."

"We'll put in a few good words for our city when she comes on Friday!"

CHAPTER 24

"You've been pretty quiet since you went out with Carrie on Monday." Maria looked over at Lisa with concern.

The stoplight ahead turned orange and then red. Lisa stopped and turned a little to face her mom. Thoughts had been spinning through her head for the past few days and she didn't know what was what.

"Well... I guess something's changing with me but I don't really know what it is yet. So I haven't really had the words to say anything."

"Could you try?"

She smiled. "Yes Mom, I can try. It's two things really. Getting to know Liam and Thea is the first one. I love those kids. They're unique, and fun, and challenging... and that moment when Liam realized I was on his side. It makes me feel so good when he comes over to the complex to chat, or texts me when something happens at school. I want to keep that connection."

The light changed, and she started driving. They were on their way to a group exercise class for Maria. Lisa drove there so often she didn't need to think about where to go.

"And, of course, having Thea choose to accept me in her world. I mean, that's a huge deal! And I love any chance to hang out with her and try to connect."

She slowed for a school zone and watched all the kids playing in the snow on their lunch break. Had she ever just played in the snow as a child? She couldn't remember.

"But it was really the weekend with Matthew and Katie that did me in. Or brought me out? I don't really know how... and I don't want to do anything that will take away from your quality of life... but I want kids in my life. Somehow."

"Kids? Not a husband?"

"Uh... I guess I'm not totally closed off to that idea anymore. But that's not the big thing for me. The big thing is kids. And Carrie pointed out on Monday that I don't need a guy to have kids. Which was a huge revelation, but it left me feeling even more confused in some ways."

She pulled into a handicapped spot at the small recreation center where the classes were held and hung up the blue handicapped card that she insisted Maria get a few months ago.

Turning to her mom, she smiled apologetically, "Sorry, that's so vague and weird and... unexpected."

Maria reached for her hand, "I should have seen it. You're so good with kids. Becky when they lived with us, and of course Alex, and Liam and Thea, and Matthew and Katie. You know, I've never wanted you to get stuck in a bad marriage like I did. But I would wish on you a thousand times the chance to be a mom."

"And you'll survive having kids in the house at some point?" Lisa teased. She knew her mom thrived in a busy house.

"I'll figure it out! Now let's get me into my exercise class so I can bulk up before kids come!"

Lisa got out and went around to the trunk to get the wheelchair out.

The area was carefully cleared of snow, and salt was sprinkled around the entrance. She noticed things like that all the time now. Being able to easily wheel her mom places was a luxury she never took for granted. And maybe soon Carrie's mom could take advantage of it too.

As she prepared for their 'dance' into the wheelchair, she brought up Carrie's mom. "You'll have to talk up all the places in the city that are easy for wheelchairs. It's time for her to have some fun exploring instead of being stuck at home all the time."

"I'd love to have her living here! We could be like a wheelchair gang together!"

Lisa rolled her eyes as she pushed her mom into the center. She left her in a large room where other people with various stages of rheumatoid arthritis met to work through exercises guided by a physiotherapist. The exercises were essential to keeping mobility, but Lisa knew it was the visiting afterward with people who were going through similar things that gave her mom a lift every time she went.

She went back to the car to get her backpack and crossed the street to the community library where she set up at one of the tables to get an hour and a half of work done before her mom needed her again.

As a teenager, Lisa only went to the school library for extra tutoring. Reading was a struggle for her, and libraries were full of books she'd never get through. But they were also the place to get enough help to pass her high school classes. After that, the library became a place to access free internet and computers when she first moved to the city.

A preschool group was there for storytime, and their excited chatter could be heard throughout the open area as they settled in. When the librarian started reading they all quieted down, caught up in a story about a little sea turtle.

Lisa opened her laptop to work and wondered what it would be like to be one of the moms bringing kids to a library.

CHAPTER 25

"OK, so I'm just picking up the lasagna and tiramisu from Luciano's? Nothing else?" Lisa called as she reached down to put on her boots.

"That's all!" Maria called from the kitchen. "By the time you get back, Jaz will either have succeeded at cooking pasta or started a fire!"

"Hey!" Jaz protested weakly. It was common knowledge that she was terrible in the kitchen at anything beyond pureeing Alex's food, but Maria and Lisa kept trying to help her learn some basic skills.

Lisa smiled as she walked out the door. At the rate Jaz was going with her business she'd be able to hire a personal chef soon. Her smile faded. But that also meant that Jaz would soon be ready to move out. Not just into the basement suite, but into her own place. Maybe they'd get another six months or a year of having the two of them in the same house, but Lisa knew there'd be a time when Jaz would want her own place.

She thought about her unconventional life as she drove to the restaurant. Moving her mom in with her was an unexpected twist in her life plan, but the best decision she ever made. Even though they'd never change the years they lived together when Lisa was young and Maria avoided any sort of connection, they definitely had their quality time together now. Would it be possible to somehow have a child *and* continue being a good caregiver for her mom? And how did she want to have kids? Those were questions she didn't even know how to go about answering.

It was only when she had a huge tray of lasagna in the back of the car along with the tiramisu that she remembered she'd be seeing Aaron shortly for the first time since her big reveal about her feelings for him. She felt her heart beat faster at the thought.

Do I regret telling him? No! What's the point of life and friends if you don't tell them really important things like you've fallen in love with them? Her cheeks warmed at the memory of his shocked look. *On the other hand, maybe I should have kept that to myself. It's definitely too late to take it back now!*

She struggled to open the front door, armed with the lasagna, and noticed a strange smell. Kicking off her boots, she walked into the kitchen and was greeted by a sheepish looking Jaz.

"The good news is the pasta for the kids is ready!" she said, gesturing to a large pot sitting on a hot pad on the counter.

"OK... what's the smell?"

"Well, I may have spilled some of it on the burner and forgot to turn the burner off."

"Burned pasta! Oh, that's what the smell is! I guess we can light some candles or something." Alex banged his spoon on the highchair tray and Lisa looked over. "But apparently it's edible!"

"I don't know whether we should get this girl cooking lessons before she moves out, or make sure she doesn't have access to anything with a burner!" Maria teased.

"Hello! Anyone home?" Carrie's voice called from the front door.

Lisa made sure the lasagna was safely on the counter before running to the door she had left open. Carrie, Jonathan, and the kids were already making their way inside. "Come in! Oh my gosh you two, I think Disneyland put some sparkle in your eyes." She hugged Katie and Matthew and reminded herself not to comment about them growing—even though they had. Kids didn't like to be told they were growing all the time, did they? "Make yourselves at home. I just need to grab dessert from the car. Oh, where are your parents Carrie?"

"They'll be here any minute. Dad wanted to drive around a few neighborhoods, first."

Lisa brushed off Jonathan's offer to help and slipped her boots back on. After quickly plugging in the car to charge, she went around to get the tiramisu only to see Aaron, Liam, and Thea turn onto the driveway. He must have parked around the corner. She paused and looked at them for a moment. Aaron still towered over Thea, who was small for her age. But Liam was now getting close to his dad's shoulder in height. Both of them were wearing gray puff jackets, and Aaron wore a red-checkered scarf wrapped around his neck. Thea wore a heavy fleece blanket wrapped around herself and Lisa guessed it was the only thing Aaron could convince her to bundle up with. Thea didn't like tight things like jacket sleeves around her arms.

"Hey you guys!" she called with a smile. There was a moment when Aaron looked right in her eyes and she felt the connection that could be there between them. But it seemed to pass before he noticed.

"Hello there! Need a hand with anything?"

"Nope, this is it. Come on in! Carrie and the kids are here already." She looked up to see more people parking. "And everyone else is following you!"

Adults and kids piled their outerwear on Maria's bed and made their way into the kitchen, dining room, and living room. Lisa loved the feeling that came from everyone visiting, laughing, and catching up on each other's lives.

"OK!" Maria called from the spot she always claimed in the dining room that gave her the best view of the entire area. "If we can all just shush for a moment… thank you!" Becky interrupted her, tapping her hand on the arm of the wheelchair and then signing 'eat' forcefully. Maria nodded to Becky before turning back to the group. "Becky's right, we need to eat! But I wanted to say a little grace, first."

After a moment's pause, everyone bowed their heads.

"Dear God," Maria began in a strong voice, "I just wanted to thank you for all these wonderful people here. And for the delicious food, and for anyone who might join our lovely circle of friends. Bless them all, Amen."

Lisa opened her eyes and looked at her mom. Did she know something Lisa didn't know? The busyness of making sure everyone got their food and drinks occupied her hands, but her mind was full of questions.

After she made sure everyone had a plate of food, she helped herself and found an empty chair beside Mr. Martin.

"My first time eating at Luciano's was when I was 24," he began. "I had been trying to get the courage to ask out Loretta for months, and then she mentioned how much she loved Italian food and I practically hollered out an invitation to Luciano's." His eyes glistened. "We went there every year for our anniversary, except for the last one."

Lisa knew he had done everything humanly possible to save his wife from cancer. In the end, he spent his life savings and still lost her. She reached out and put her hand on his arm, "That's a lot of years of eating Italian food together."

He smiled, "Forty-three years. I'm a lucky man."

The conversation flowed around them, but Lisa sat quietly beside him, waiting. She had gotten to know him quite well over the past few months and knew he'd find someone to tell a story to after the wave of grief over losing his wife eased. Until then, she'd stay beside him.

"Mr. Martin!" Liam called from across the room as he walked over with Matthew. "Can you make a solar panel that powers a computer? Matthew and I are doing a science project."

Lisa stood up to make room for the two boys to sit beside him. That was the thing about kids. Life was never predictable! Aaron was already in the kitchen tidying up. He looked up when she came in.

"Hi."

"Hi."

"How have you been?" He turned back to the sink where he was rinsing dishes before loading them into the dishwasher.

Lisa looked around for Thea before answering.

"She's in your mom's room with the iPad," he said with a smile.

"OK. So, I've been OK. Um, you know… keeping busy. You?"

He sighed. "I feel really bad about the other week. I took off on you. And—"

They were interrupted by Jonathan coming in with a stack of dishes. "Man, that lasagna was amazing Lisa! We're going to have to add Luciano's to our favorite eating list! Where do you want these dishes?"

"If you put them here, I'll scrape them and Aaron can keep on loading. Make sure everyone who wants seconds gets them."

"Well, between Matthew and Liam I think all the leftovers will be gone in a few hours." He put his hand on Aaron's shoulder and leaned forward, "Do you remember eating *that* much when you were their age? I'm beginning to think I didn't put a big enough fridge in our kitchen!"

Aaron looked back and smiled, "Doesn't matter how big the fridge is, they'll still complain about having nothing to eat!"

"Well, we'll divide anything that's left between the two of you," Lisa offered.

"That should take us past midnight, at least!" Jonathan joked. "I'll go round up more dishes."

"He's a different man now that he's married."

Lisa nodded her head, afraid to say anything.

"Find someone like him, Lisa. You deserve that. I… I just can't…" He paused, and then turned to face her. "I can't be that man for you but I've got your back when you find him."

She felt her eyes start to feel hot and dry and wondered for a moment if she might start crying in front of him. Slowly she took a deep breath and let it out. A part of her knew that this would happen. Relief about being right competed with sadness over knowing there wouldn't be any room in her heart for a guy who wasn't Aaron.

"I wonder… well… I guess I don't know what's next for me."

"Nothing but good things Lisa. That's what you deserve."

Together they cleaned up the rest of the dishes and Lisa got everyone set up with dessert. For the kids who didn't want tiramisu she handed out ice cream bars. Liam, Matthew, and Cherish all asked if they could have both.

Once she checked on all her guests, she went into her mom's room. She almost couldn't see Thea behind the pile of coats, scarves, and gloves.

"Hey you," she whispered as she got on the bed beside Thea. At first, there wasn't even an acknowledgement that she was there. Thea held the iPad in front of her face, watching an episode of BBC Earth. As Sir David Attenborough's soothing voice played, Lisa watched Thea. As usual, her hair was in a halo around her head. There was a very subtle smell of conditioner and Lisa knew this meant Aaron had spent hours coaxing Thea to have a bath and let him wash and care for her hair. She resisted the urge to reach out and smooth it back. Thea hated having her hair touched.

After a few minutes, Thea briefly touched Lisa's arm with a single finger and then pointed to a bee on the screen. The acknowledgment of Lisa's presence and the offer to include her made her feel so special.

"Looks like those bees are really working hard. And I love those flowers! We should plant some of those in the spring—whatever they are."

Thea looked up at Lisa and nodded her head once before going back to her show and Lisa went back to her guests. Thea would likely stay there until Aaron came to get her. It was a good sign that she felt calm at their house.

By eleven the house was quiet. Lisa popped in to check on her mom before heading to bed.

"It was a good idea to have everyone over!"

Maria nodded from her bed where she was propped up against some pillows. She looked tired but very content. "We have to keep on doing that. Having people over. It's so easy for lots of time to pass and suddenly we're all disconnected."

"Hey, I didn't even get a chance to talk to Carrie's parents! Did you?"

"Oh yes, for quite a while! I don't think there's any more convincing to be done. This sick spell really frightened Julia, and she wants to have all the time with Matthew and Katie that she can."

"So they're moving here?"

"Well, I think so. They don't want to live with Carrie and Jonathan —they *are* newlyweds after all—so there are some things to figure out."

"Too bad our basement suite isn't accessible. That would give them a place to stay until they find something. And the accessible suite at the housing project is just too small for two people…"

"I gave them Frank's number. He'll be able to find them a place."

"True! After all, he found this place, and the project for us! Talk about a real estate agent straight from heaven! Anyways, you're dozing off as we talk. Time to get some sleep, Mom."

"I will. Thanks for tonight, Lisa."

Lisa leaned in to gently hug her mom and give her a kiss on the cheek, "You're welcome. I love you."

"I love you too."

CHAPTER 26

The sounds of Alex chattering away in baby talk woke Lisa up the next morning. She popped her head into the room Jaz shared with Alex to say 'good morning' before heading downstairs to start her day.

She brought her coffee and a travel mug with tea for her mom into the bedroom and got in bed beside her. They started having Saturday mornings in bed together a few months ago when their schedules allowed. It was one of Lisa's favorite times in her week.

"Well, if I could have a houseful of people here every night, I'd definitely get caught up on sleep! I always sleep better after being around people."

"Were you this much of a social butterfly before you met Dad?"

"Me? No! I was practically afraid of my own shadow! I don't know where this part of me comes from!"

"Doesn't matter, as long as you're happy now."

"I am. Are you?"

Lisa looked at her mom, debating how much to share. She thought back to Carrie's mom having a health scare and wanting to be as close to family as possible now. "I'm going to be. I mean, I'm going to be happy again. So..." she rolled her eyes. "Turns out I've fallen in love with Aaron."

A burst of laughter came from somewhere and she clamped her hand over her mouth. "I can't believe I just laughed about it! Because I told him, and he's totally not interested."

"Oh, Lisa. I'm so sorry! I should have guessed. You just light up when you're around him. But you've never been interested in men so I missed it. I'm so sorry!"

"You said that already. It's not your fault. It's not anyone's fault. And I'm kind of really weirded out by the whole thing."

"Are you sure he's not interested? Did he tell you?"

"Yeah. He did. I should have known. He hasn't told me in so many words, but I think his ex-wife took his heart and crushed it. You know he cares so deeply about everyone—look at how he is with his kids! When she left it must have been beyond horrible for him."

"That doesn't mean he can't try again!"

"I know, Mom. But I think for him it means he won't risk another relationship. And I don't want to be with anyone if it's not him."

"So what's next then?"

"I don't know. I know there *is* a next for me. It's kinda my thing to always go for something more—you know that. But this time I don't know what that is. I think it involves kids though."

"Kids? Without a man?"

"Yeah. It is the 21st century! We can do it all!"

"Like, you'd go buy some sperm?"

"Mom! No!" she laid her head back against the wall. "Well, I don't think so. I really don't want to be pregnant. And I don't think babies are even my thing except for Alex, and Jaz does all the hard stuff with him so that doesn't really count…"

"Whatever you decide, I'll support you. At least, as best as I can. I can't do much physically. But I've got time and money." She giggled. "Time and money — I'm really pretty lucky, aren't I?"

Lisa wanted to disagree with her mom. She *wasn't* lucky! She had lost the best years of her life to an abusive husband and now that she could have a good life, arthritis prevented it. But she nodded and forced herself to smile.

"So, what should we do today? I've had a great night's sleep, the house is clean, and there aren't any meetings scheduled for Jaz's company."

"I don't know. It's winter! There's nothing *to* do! And I'm totally caught up on work, so that's out."

They looked at each other. "The mall!" they both said at once. After years of never having money, both of them loved the freedom of going to the mall, just in case they found something to buy.

"OK, I'll get dressed and see if Jaz wants to come. And then we can eat and head out. Do you need any help before I go?"

"I don't think so. Check in when you're dressed if I'm not out."

Lisa ran up the stairs, laughing to herself at how excited she got over the idea of a trip to the mall. She hadn't had any friends in high school, and in her small town there wasn't a decent mall to go to even if she ever had the chance to 'hang out'. Now, she still felt a little thrill that she could go somewhere and buy what she wanted when she wanted to.

CHAPTER 27

The mall parking lot was busy, and Lisa couldn't find a handicapped spot. Finally, she pulled into a loading zone and used the space to unload the wheelchair and the stroller. Once Jaz was out with Alex in the stroller and Maria in her wheelchair Lisa drove off to find parking. They'd have to do the same thing all over again in reverse when it was time to leave and she wondered if petitioning the mall for more handicapped spaces would do any good.

When they finally made it around to the entrance, they realized what all the fuss was about. Christmas shopping was in full swing, and it seemed like everyone had come out to get started on their lists.

"Oh, I just love seeing all the decorations up!" Maria exclaimed.

"They're the same ones they have every year Mom."

"Doesn't matter. It still makes me feel happy! And this year we can go all out for Alex!"

"My mom has already booked some sort of professional Santa pictures for him next week. Apparently the mall Santa isn't good enough for him!" Jaz reached down and started taking Alex's jacket off.

"Tell her I'd like a copy of them, if she doesn't mind."

"Of course! Hey, what are all those trees there? That's different!"

Lisa and Jaz walked side by side to the elaborately decorated Christmas trees, pushing the wheelchair and stroller.

"A Very Charitable Christmas," Maria read off the sign. "Oh, all the charities have decorated a tree, and we can vote for our favorite by putting donations in the boxes in front of each one. Well, I am going to give each one a donation! But let's look at them all first."

As they walked around, exclaiming over all the creative ways the trees were decorated, they came to one tree that was just a simple evergreen with a star on the top. A sign credited a foster parent organization with the tree. In front was a basket with ornament-shaped cards. Another sign explained their project:

Please help us decorate our tree! Each ornament card represents a wish from a foster child in our system. Choose a card, purchase the wish, and leave it unwrapped under the tree. Then, put the 'ornament' on our tree. We hope to have a tree full of wishes by Christmas Eve!

"Grab a bunch, Lisa! We'll go shopping right now!"

Lisa loved to see her mom excited, and she was happy to do some shopping for someone else. "OK. Why don't we grab some coffees and read through the wishes? There are probably some things that we can get at the same stores."

"Coffees? We just got here! Not that I'm complaining. I could definitely go for a candy cane mocha! And I can feed Alex now so he's ready for a nap when we're shopping."

They waited for a wheelchair accessible table to open up, and then they all eagerly started looking through the cards.

"Oh. It's not what I expected." Maria held open the card for the others to see. "Backpack for a five-year-old girl," she read. "Not very magical if you ask me."

"Well, we could get a backpack and fill it with lots of fun stuff!" Lisa suggested.

"And what about this one? Pajamas, socks, and underwear for a ten-year-old boy. That's not what boys are asking for on their Christmas lists! I'm calling them up!"

Lisa and Jaz exchanged bemused looks while Maria looked up the phone number for the organization and called them.

"Hello? Yes, my name is Maria, and I'm at the mall right now looking at your 'wish' cards. The ones we can shop for? I'm having trouble thinking of these things as real wishes. Backpacks? Under-wear?" she paused and listening as the person on the other end talked. "Oh. I see... Don't the foster parents give them things like that?... Hmm... And what if we put a few extra things in with each wish? Will they get to that child?... Alright. We'll see what we can do... You're welcome."

She hung up and looked at the two women. "Well, he said they are all real wishes from real children. Apparently, when kids come into the system, they often don't have anything with them except what they're wearing. And it sounds like the foster parents—some of them at least—can't be constantly buying basics for the kids. I mean, this is just terrible! These kids must feel so lost in a stranger's home and they don't even have their own backpack to take to school!"

It was hard to know what to say. None of them had ever thought about foster kids who spent Christmas away from home. "I wonder if they're glad to be away from home, or if it's worse to be away." Lisa looked down at her latte. When she left home at 18, she chose what to bring with her. It wasn't much, but she had the basics and a few treasures like pictures of her grandparents. She would have felt lone-lier without them. "What do you want to do, Mom?"

"Well, we can get the things on the list, but let's try to do more than that for each child. Look, there's a copy of each wish that goes with the gift, so we can hope that those kids *will* get the extras. We'll just have to guess at what each child might like. I wonder what happens when these children have birthdays in their foster homes? Do they still wish for things like underwear? Do their foster parents celebrate?"

"Sounds like you need a visit with that organization! You can get them all sorted out!" Jaz joked.

"Maybe I will. It's just not something I've ever thought about, and now I feel terrible for those children!"

"At least this is one time where shopping can help! Let's look at all of these and figure out which stores to go to."

They shopped, stopped for a late lunch, and then shopped some more. By the end of the day they were exhausted, Alex was more than done with being in the stroller, and a pile of gifts sat under the foster parent tree. When Lisa put the last bag of gifts down, they all took a minute to look at everything.

The ten-year-old boy's request for pajamas, socks, and underwear included a LEGO set, some brain teaser puzzles, and a baseball and glove.

The five-year-old girl's backpack had a coloring book and crayons, a stuffed animal, and a dress-up set with a tiara and a sparkly skirt.

A 15-year-old boy's wish for a notebook and pen also included a science-themed daily calendar, a warm hat and scarf, and a gift card for the large bookstore in the mall.

A toddler boy's wish for a truck became a set of trucks, a stuffed animal, and a board book about trucks.

A 17-year-old girl's wish for makeup had a makeup set and brushes, a set of travel accessories, and a book with cute sayings all in a mini backpack similar to the ones every teenage girl seemed to carry around the mall.

They also found two cards for nine-year-old twin brothers that each asked for a hat and gloves. The ladies bought coordinating hats, gloves, scarves, and hoodies for each brother plus a basketball for one and a soccer ball for the other.

The final wish was bittersweet for Jaz to shop for. A 17-year-old girl wished for 'baby things'. They bought diapers, wipes, onesies, some gender-neutral outfits, a pacifier and burp clothes, a journal to track a baby's first year, and some scented hand lotion for the young mom.

"It's hard to imagine what she must be feeling," Jaz said as they drove away from the mall. "Plus, I don't even know if you can keep a baby if you're in foster care yourself. Would they take it away?"

"I can't imagine them doing anything like that!" Maria exclaimed.

"You know, even at 18, I wasn't really thinking about how to take care of a baby. If it wasn't for you all throwing that baby shower for me and everyone helping me out, it would have been so much harder."

"And here you are, not even a year after Alex's birth with the money and ability to set up a teenage mom you don't even know with the things she'll need for her baby!"

"That part's cool, for sure," Jaz agreed. "But it's not much compared to what she's going to need."

"I hope it helps those children feel a little better over Christmas!" Maria was beginning to feel her arthritis. "And now I feel like Alex, ready to get my body into a different position. Although I'll put my feet up in my recliner, and he'll want to tear around the house!

CHAPTER 28

The foster parent agency's office was in a run-down strip mall in a neighborhood Lisa and Maria had never been to before. The doorway was too narrow for Maria's wheelchair, so she had to stand up and shuffle through, and then wait for Lisa to fold the wheelchair, bring it into the office, and open it again for Maria to sit in. It was the first time they hadn't been able to get the wheelchair into a public building and Lisa was shocked.

"How can you get away with not having a place accessible in a mall?" she wondered out loud.

"It's something we've been trying to change for years." A man in his early thirties walked into the small waiting area. He wore a faded blue button-up shirt and khaki pants that were bunched around his ankles. His dark brown hair was neatly trimmed, and he looked tired. He reached out his hand to each of them. "Hi, I'm Mark. You must be the ladies who called to ask about the Christmas tree."

"Yes, I'm Maria, and this is my daughter Lisa." They both shook his hand.

"I'd invite you into my office, but the door frame is just as narrow so we'll have to meet here."

"How can you have an office that's not accessible? Don't people with strollers need to come in too?"

He pointed to a plastic bin beside the front door that held bike locks. "If the stroller doesn't fit through the door, the parents can borrow a bike lock and secure it out there. It's the best we can do."

"Doesn't the city know this is a code violation?"

"The company that leases the office is always threatening to raise the rent. I'm careful not to do anything that might upset them. We can't afford anyplace else." He shifted in his chair. "But what can I do for you?"

"Why don't you start by telling us about your organization?" Lisa asked. "My mom and I don't really know anything about it, except that you have kids who are wishing for very basic things for Christmas."

He smiled before answering. "That tree was the idea of one of our foster moms. In the past, we've managed to gather some used books and toys to give the kids. Having them each list a wish and then trying to make them come true is quite ambitious, but it's a great idea!"

"Anyways... we're a small non-profit organization that handles the placement of up to fifty foster children at a time. We have a full-time social worker, as well as myself—I'm a licensed counselor and social worker—and my wife helps me with the administration. She's a hairdresser."

He paused for a moment, as if he was trying to decide what to tell them. "I formed this organization because I wanted a higher standard for foster children. But the fact is, there are too many children in need of care and we simply can't give them what they need— services beyond foster parenting that might help them get the start they need in life. I have wonderful foster parents working for me, and I do everything I can to be there for them and the kids. But we're just overwhelmed all the time."

Lisa looked around the small waiting room. If he had any resources, he sure wasn't spending them on décor. She looked at her mom. What next?

Maria seemed to read her expression. "What do you need for these kids and their foster parents?"

"Well, we're always looking for quality foster parents." He looked down for a moment. "I have a rather intense training program. I think it scares away all but the most determined. But I'm not willing to compromise. The government is always asking me to take on more cases, but I just can't.

"Most of the kids that are placed with us end up doing really well for the most part. If I could pay foster parents what they're worth, we wouldn't need a tree up in the mall. As you saw, the kids don't ask for much. Like I mentioned on the phone, the kids often come into the system with just the clothes on their back. Or they have their belongings shoved in a garbage bag."

Maria gasped. "No! That must make them feel like they're not worth anything!"

He nodded, "Like trash, to be exact. But there's not much that can be done when a child's at immediate risk. That's why backpacks mean so much to the kids. It gives them something that belongs to them. Something nice. And something that they can easily take with them if they have to move again."

Lisa felt like she needed time to think about everything. Her mom looked at her, but she just shook her head, not sure what to say.

"Thanks for meeting with us Mark. I guess we just need some time to think about what you've told us. Well, maybe you could do one thing... if you have any of those ornament wish lists left over will you call me? I don't want any of your kids to be without a gift this Christmas."

His face broke out in a huge smile. "Yes! Of course, that's wonderful! We do tend to divide things up so every child gets *something*. This would save us from doing that. Can I put your contact info down then?"

After sharing both their numbers, they had to repeat the stand and shuffle to get Maria and her wheelchair out of the office. But the time they were back in the car, Maria was out of breath.

"I can't quite process the whole foster child thing right now," Lisa said as she pointed the car towards home, "but I *am* going to do something about the accessibility of that mall! There's no way an owner should be allowed to get away with that."

CHAPTER 29

For the next week, Lisa took every spare minute to call the owners of the strip mall and remind them of their obligation to make every unit accessible. After a few days of being given the runaround, she managed to get the number of the owner.

She called every morning and afternoon, leaving messages describing the problem and how they could fix it. As the days went on, she added more information to each message.

"I think I'm becoming an expert in accessibility law and our local bylaws," she informed everyone during dinner. "I really don't know if anyone's listening to my messages or not. I wonder if it's time for a face-to-face meeting? I haven't had one of those since I was working for Golden Lion."

"What were those for?" Jaz asked.

"Well, there were a few tenants who weren't making their lease payments on time. So I went to each of their offices and let them know they needed to get their accounts up to date." She smiled at the memory. "Actually, I really enjoyed it! I guess there's a part of me that's a secret enforcer or something."

"Just the thought of that makes me feel stressed! I'll leave the confrontations to you and stick to making clothes. I got a great deal on eBay today, so watch out for a big delivery coming sometime next week."

"I can't believe you haven't run out of ideas yet! I have a hard time putting together an outfit every morning and here you are, still creating new clothes out of old ones." There was no mistaking the pride in Maria's voice.

"I feel like every idea I have creates two more new ideas. I actually quit scrolling through Instagram because it gave me too many ideas! Now I just post the clothes for sale and get back out."

"It looks like you're seeing a steady increase in sales in the past week and a half. Do you think it's Christmas shopping?" Lisa loved checking on Jaz's sales numbers—something Jaz often forgot about.

"Yep! Lots more dress clothes going out. I could use someone to manage the inventory and listings for me. It's taking at least an hour a day…" her voice trailed off and Lisa and Maria both looked at her.

Finally, Lisa decided to deal with the thing they all wanted to avoid. "I think you need more space, too."

Maria sighed. "Do we have to have this conversation? I'd rather just keep you right here Jaz, even though that's selfish."

Jaz reached over and lifted Alex out of his highchair. She held him close against her. "I feel like I'm about to change everything and I don't want to. I want you guys right here with Alex and I for everything. And I know we talked about me moving to the basement suite."

"But…" Lisa prompted.

"But, I really want to live somewhere I can have a studio, and be close enough for Alex to go to Mandarin daycare and then preschool."

"What?! No way! Are you serious?" Lisa had a hard time believing

Jaz would give in to her parents' demands. They had been pushing Mandarin preschool for Alex since the day they met him.

"It's totally weird, right? I mean, at first I didn't want to do anything they said because I didn't want Alex being raised like I was raised. But there's this other part of me that's so proud of my heritage, and I don't want to take that away from him."

"These are some big decisions."

Jaz nodded at Maria. "A part of me has been ignoring all this. But there's another part of me that feels like I want to do it really badly."

"If this is what you want, then we totally support it. How can we help?"

"Oh Maria, you've totally rescued me already! I mean, taking me in, and helping me start the business, and all the help with Alex. It's been amazing, and I'm so grateful for you both."

"Not to mention the fact that you would have starved to death if we left you to your own devices in a kitchen!" Lisa added wryly.

"I'll get a rice cooker!"

"You and Alex will live on rice?"

Jaz smiled and cuddled Alex even closer. "Honestly? I think we'll be eating a lot of takeout until my Mom figures out that I need her to cook for me. Then we'll be just fine!"

"I'm really excited for you. And a little jealous. You know what you want next and you'll get it! I just wish I knew what was next for me."

"Well... I was hoping you could work with me on-site for a couple half days every week? There will be a lot more negotiations and accounting with each new line of accessible clothing. And I'll need help finding the right people to hire." She laughed, "Oh, and then I'll need you to fire anyone that's no good. You can do all that, right?"

Lisa smiled, "Of course. Everything you need. And I'll be happy to come play with numbers at your studio whenever you want."

"What will you do with the rooms here? You could Airbnb our bedroom, but the sewing room isn't really good for anything on its own."

"I'm not sure yet. I have vague thoughts in my head after our meeting with that foster parenting director. But nothing certain yet. It seems like you've got all the definite plans in the house right now."

Later that night Lisa sat in bed with a yellow lined notepad in her lap. She started to write her ideas out:

- *buy more apartments for affordable housing*
- *foster parent*
- *adopt*
- *grow bookkeeping business*
- *travel*
- *Airbnb more rooms*
- *online dating*

Do all of them? Do none of them? Go crazy trying to figure out her life? Her phone buzzed and she reached over to turn it off. Normally she put it on silent when she got ready for bed. The text was from Liam:

> *hey. so cherish is crapping out at school. u told me once that school was hard for u. can u make her feel better?*
>
> *Hey back! I don't know, but I can try.*
>
> *cool! i'll make her come to our house after school tomorrow and you can come over. k?*

Lisa smiled at Liam's response. He was definitely a kid that got things done!

Sure. See you tomorrow after school.

She wondered how it would feel to be in Aaron's house. Although he'd be at work, she knew he'd have something delicious in the crockpot for dinner, and she would feel his presence everywhere. A part of her already regretted agreeing to Liam's plan, but there was no way she would back out. Maybe she could take Cherish out for hot chocolate or something.

CHAPTER 30

Lisa's heart sank when she pulled up beside Aaron's house. His car was there, and that meant he was home. With a big breath and a mental head shake, she walked up the pathway and knocked on the door. Aaron opened it.

"Lisa! Liam just told me he invited you over. Come on in!"

"Invited me? More of an instruction to show up, but I'm happy to be here." She surprised herself by realizing she *was* happy to be there. Aaron's house was full of good feelings for her. She loved watching him interact with his kids and move around the kitchen with ease. It was such a contrast to her own childhood. "Why are you home early?"

"Daycare operator got appendicitis! So she has to close everything down for the next week to have surgery and recover."

Lisa knew the special needs daycare that picked Thea up after school was a lifeline for Aaron. "How will you manage?"

"I'm not sure. It just happened this morning. If it was any other time I could leave work early every day to pick up Thea from school. But here are some massive changes happening at work right now and I need to be in the office… I still have to figure it out."

"Let me help!" she blurted out before she could stop herself. "I've done everything with her except driving. If she can tolerate that, then I can pick her up and stay here until you can leave work." She suddenly cared a little less about her feelings for Aaron. He was a friend who needed help, and she was one of the only people in his world that Thea didn't mind.

He paused and seemed to be having an internal argument with himself. "Uh…." he started.

"It's from one friend to another. Nothing more. OK?"

"What about your mom? Doesn't she have appointments?"

Lisa shook her head. "Everything's in the mornings for her."

His shoulders sagged in relief. "That would be amazing. Thank you! I'll pay you of course."

"Riiight. Not going to happen Aaron."

"I thought I'd try. OK, how about I send you home with supper every night?"

"Now *that* is something I can't say no to! But for today, I've been summoned to chat with Cherish…"

"Downstairs in the TV room."

The basement was a vintage sanctuary for Aaron and his kids, complete with the original wood paneling. In the TV room, an over-stuffed couch and bean bag chairs invited everyone to sink in for hours of relaxing. In the corner was a weight set where Aaron could work out while keeping an eye on the kids.

As soon as Liam saw her, he jumped up from the couch. "Cool, you're here!" He muted the TV that had some sort of teen sitcom on. "You guys talk. I'll go hang out with Dad."

Lisa watched him run upstairs and then turned to Cherish. She smiled apologetically. "Guess I have my instructions." Sitting down on the couch, she turned and faced Cherish. Normally an outgoing, strong-willed girl, Cherish had been put in a foster home when she and her mom were evicted from their apartment. She fought fiercely against the system until they were reunited when Lisa set them up with a housing plan they could afford. Although Cherish was still strong-willed, Lisa hoped she had calmed down some in the past few months.

"How's the apartment treating you?" she started.

Cherish looked up from the TV. Her normally bouncy dark wavy hair looked limp and out of place without her typical ponytail. She had her hands tucked into the sleeves of an oversized sweatshirt, and her leggings and socks were stretched out and baggy.

"The house is good. Mom's super happy. She's gonna get a Christmas tree soon."

"You don't look like you're very happy. And I'm guessing it's not because you hate Christmas. Tell me about school."

Cherish took a deep breath and let it out slowly. "Before we lived here, when I ran away all the time, it was OK to suck at school because I was a foster kid and I always skipped school. But now I go, like, every day. And I still suck at everything. Liam and Matthew are super smart and they're always trying to beat each other at tests…" She crossed her arms and tucked her legs up. For a tall girl, she could make herself surprisingly small.

"I sucked at school too. Big time."

"Yeah, Liam told me. But you're rich now and you have your own business so it's not the same."

"The one thing I was really good at—*am* really good at—" she corrected herself, "is numbers. Math. But reading's really really hard for me. It takes forever and I don't understand things very easily."

"Are you, like, dyslexic or something?"

"I don't think so. I just can't read very well. But I didn't have any friends in school so I wasn't around smart people like you are. I was really scared of failing high school, and being trapped living at home." Lisa paused, wondering if Cherish would even be interested in her story. She figured it wouldn't hurt to tell her a bit. "My dad was really really mean. He told me that as soon as I graduated I'd get a job and finally start paying him back for everything he had to do for me. I knew if I stayed at home I'd never escape. So I did every-thing I could to graduate. I asked all of my teachers for help. I was so embarrassed. Every day I'd need them to explain the homework to me again after class got out because I could never figure it out by reading. Then I'd go to the library and get help from the student tutors."

"I'd die if I had to get help from other students."

Lisa nodded, "It was so humiliating. They were all super nice and helpful, though. I ran away too. Just like you. The day of my high school graduation. I didn't even say goodbye to my mom because I was so mad that she didn't come to my graduation. I worked so hard for it, but they didn't know."

"She's nice now."

"She was always nice, but my dad had her trapped and she was too afraid to be herself. I still feel really lucky that we got a second chance at having a relationship. Does your mom know about how you're doing in school?"

Cherish shook her head. "She's working a lot right now and I... um... I kinda put my phone number down as the school contact number. So she doesn't get any calls. I don't want her to worry."

"Sounds to me like you've got some killer problem-solving skills!"

"You mean, like being sneaky?"

"Sort of. You saw a problem—your mom finding out about your

schoolwork—and you figured out a way to avoid it by giving the school your number instead of hers. I may not agree with what you're doing, but you *are* trying to fix something. What if you looked at your schoolwork the same way? As a problem you need to figure out?"

"I won't cheat. I'd rather fail than cheat."

"See? I totally agree with you now! What else can you do to fix things?" She was genuinely curious to hear what Cherish would come up with.

"Well... if I *hear* stuff I learn it better. Sometimes I pretend I'm zoning out during class projects, but I'm listening to everyone else talking about it. And then I can figure out what we're supposed to do. Sometimes."

"Holy cow! That's smart!"

Cherish smiled, "I like being sneaky like that." Her smiled faded. "But then I can't show that I get it. If the teacher asks a question, I can answer it. But nobody gives tests where you answer out loud."

"Yet."

"Huh?"

"Nobody gives tests where you answer out loud *yet*."

"Do you think I should ask to talk the test?"

"Do you want to?"

She sat up, "Oh yeah. That would be so cool! But..." her shoulders slumped "... I don't think the teachers will let me. None of them really like me."

Lisa could see how Cherish's usually forceful way of expressing herself might rub teachers the wrong way. Especially if she didn't show up to class half the time. "OK... so maybe that's not the solution?"

"Would you have asked?"

Lisa nodded, "Definitely. If I thought I could get through my classes by taking tests out loud I would have tried it. I don't know if they would have gone for it though."

"Then I'll do it. Hey, I'm already failing, like, everything. It's not like it can get worse."

"Oh Cherish, I'm sorry. If you can figure out how to get through this, things will get better. High school isn't the best time for lots of people like you and me. But once I graduated and I could do things my way things got a lot better."

"I totally want to be like you when I grow up! And then I'll tell some other kid who's failing that life will get better!"

As if on cue, Liam came into the room with a bowl of chips and three cans of soda. He handed out the cans, pulled a bean bag up to the couch, and plopped down on it with the bowl resting where everyone could help themselves. Cherish turned the volume back up on the TV.

Lisa half watched the show, and half watched the two teens. She always thought life as a teenager was super complicated. But these two seemed perfectly content to have an answer to a problem and then move on with their day. Maybe having a supportive parent— even one that didn't really know everything that was going on with her daughter at school—made all the difference. When the show ended, she said goodbye and made her way upstairs.

CHAPTER 31

The week flew by. Lisa made sure to have all her work finished before it was time to pick up Thea. Then she did her best to replicate Aaron's approach to his daughter's needs until he came in the door from work. To her surprise, Thea didn't seem to mind having Lisa pick her up and take her home. She knew Aaron still had all the hard parts of the day—things like trying to get Thea to sleep at night and doing her hair in the morning—but it felt like she was making a difference for the family.

On the last day before Thea was set to start after school care again, Cherish flew through the front door. "Lisa!" she hollered while Thea squealed back at her and put her hands over her ears. Cherish ignored Thea. "Lisa! I did a verbal test today, and I rocked it!" She threw her arms around Lisa and nearly knocked her over with a bear hug.

"That's fantastic! What subject?"

"Math!"

Lisa thought she was joking at first. "No, really, what was it in?"

"Math! So, I went into class at lunchtime, and the teacher read out each question and then I told him how I would answer it and he wrote it down. He said I showed that I understood everything and I got an A! I've never got an A on *anything* before!"

Liam came in and slammed the door behind him. "Dang, Cherish! When did you learn to run so fast?"

She beamed at him. "I'm smart now!"

He rolled his eyes and turned to Lisa, "You see what you've done? She won't shut up now!"

"Well, it sounds like talking is her strong point so you've probably got to get used to it."

Cherish did a little dance and gave Lisa another hug. "Thanks for helping me! You should be, like, a big sister or something. You totally know stuff!"

Lisa waited for them to grab food and head downstairs before sitting beside Thea. She still held her hands over her ears and was rocking back and forth, but didn't seem too distressed. Lisa suspected she liked Cherish in her own way.

She wondered about what Cherish said. Not 'you should be a mom' but 'you should be a big sister'. It had a nice ring to it. As an only child she had often dreamed about having siblings. Jaz had definitely become a sister to her, and the thought of not having her in the house soon was kind of depressing.

There were programs where you could volunteer to hang out with a child once in a while, but she wasn't sure if it would be the same as what she did for Cherish without even meaning to.

A wet hand on her arm snapped her out of her thoughts. Thea had been sucking on her fingers and had suddenly decided she needed Lisa's attention. "Hey you. What do you want?"

Thea gave the sign Aaron created for her that meant she wanted a

'Thea hug'. Lisa carefully lifted her into her lap and wrapped her arms around her tightly. Aaron had said she didn't like light touches, and Lisa didn't know how hard to squeeze her. Thea signed 'more' and Lisa squeezed as hard as she dared. She felt the little girl relax into her, and she rested her chin on Thea's head. Whatever else she was meant to do, she'd remember this day for a long time.

CHAPTER 32

"Are you ready?" Maria asked Lisa as they waited by the front door.

Lisa shook her head 'no'. "Six weeks of training, two first aid courses, more interviews and background checks than I ever thought possible, three months of trying to get prepared for this, and I am totally freaking out right now."

"Just be yourself. Everyone likes you, and you have a way of connecting with people."

"I wish Jaz and Alex were here. She looks so hip and trendy all the time, and Alex is so adorable that everyone chills out right away."

"Lisa! This is about what you have to offer. Don't minimize it!"

They heard footsteps on the front porch and then the doorbell rang. Lisa looked at her mom. "Here we go!"

She opened the door to the now-familiar face of Mark, the director of the foster parent's organization, and a visibly pregnant teenager.

"Hello!"

Mark took a half step forward. "Lisa, Maria, this is Bethany. Bethany, meet Lisa and Maria."

Bethany looked at them defiantly for a moment, and then dropped her gaze and said, "Hey."

"Come on in, both of you!" Lisa held open the door wide. Bethany walked in with just a single worn backpack. Mark smiled and followed her in.

"Mark, why don't you follow Mom to the dining room, and I'll show Bethany her room." She turned to Bethany. "If you want to take your shoes off, and then we'll head upstairs."

While she struggled to remove her shoes without bending down or untying them, Lisa looked at her new foster child. Bethany was short, maybe just over 5 feet tall, and her protruding belly looked uncomfortable. Her ankles showed beneath sweatpants that had seen better days, and she wore an oversized plaid shirt under an open zip-up sweater. She wore her brown hair short on one side and down past her ear on the other side, ending in bleach blonde tips. When she finally got her shoes off, Lisa could see her toes poking through holes in her socks.

"Right this way. Do you want me to carry your backpack?"

"No."

Lisa tried not to walk too fast up the stairs. "So, my room's right over there, and this is your room here." She hoped the lilac bedspread and accents weren't too girly. It had seemed like a perfect bedroom for a teenage girl until Bethany walked in the door. "You have your own bathroom up here, and the other door heads into a room you can use for a nursery if you want. I had a friend staying here with her little boy until a few months ago and they used the same room, but it was pretty crowded."

Bethany dropped her backpack on the bed but didn't say anything.

"Did you need to use the bathroom or anything? I put towels and bath stuff and everything in there, but if you need anything different, just tell me."

"I'm good," was her only reply.

"OK, well, let's head downstairs then."

Lisa could hear Bethany letting out a hiss of air each time she set one foot down. It seemed like she had an injury or a disability, but Lisa didn't dare ask.

"Here, come sit beside me Bethany!" Maria said cheerfully, pulling out the chair beside her. Wordlessly the girl sat down.

"What can I get for you all to drink?" Lisa asked, moving behind the counter that separated the kitchen and dining room.

"Decaf green tea for me," Maria answered.

"Coffee," Mark said, "Always coffee for me!" He turned to Bethany, and she shrugged her shoulders.

During the time Lisa made everyone's drinks, Mark and Maria kept up a steady stream of small talk. Lisa put a glass of juice and a glass of water in front of Bethany.

When she sat down with her own coffee, Mark pulled out a file from his backpack. "Bethany already knows I have to check my notes for everything because I'm not so good with the details. Let me see… one of the first things you'll need to do is find a doctor. Bethany's former foster parents both worked full-time so she hasn't been for a check-up in quite a while. And I'll leave it to you ladies to decide how to prepare for labor and delivery."

Bethany's face visibly paled at the mention of labor and delivery. Maria reached over and patted her arm, "Don't you worry. We'll do our very best to take good care of you!" A half-smile crossed her face for a moment, the first positive emotion she had shown.

"Now," Mark continued, "we've completed the registration for online school, and I've managed to find a laptop that you can use Bethany.

I'll drop it off tomorrow morning. This is a real self-directed program, so it should work to fit it around what you feel up to doing every day."

"What about my mom?"

A strange look passed over Mark's face, and Lisa wondered what it meant. He quickly replaced it with a neutral expression.

"Right. Bethany's been trying to reach her mom for a while. If it's alright with you, she'd like to use your phone to try and call her occasionally." He turned to face her, "I know you're really anxious to connect with her. We've done all we can from our end, and I have it scheduled to call that number every week until we hear from her. Hopefully, those messages will get through."

"Sure, you can leave my number and Mom's number, just in case." Lisa wondered why Bethany didn't have her own phone. Chances are, they'd find out eventually. "And if you need to call anyone, just ask. I'm not really on my phone that much. Mom's the real social butterfly here, so it might be harder to catch her when she's not on the phone!"

Mark finished his coffee and stood up, "Well I'll leave you three now to get acquainted. If you need anything, please don't hesitate to call!"

Lisa followed him to the front door and let him out. Taking a breath in, she made her way back to the dining room.

"So, I think the most important thing to do next is find out what you like to eat! I do all the cooking around here, and I'd like to think I'm OK at it." She smiled at Bethany, "Anything you can't get enough of right now?"

"Um... I hate milk. But maybe I'm supposed to drink it anyways?"

"We can ask the doctor about that. Do you have a prenatal vitamin you're taking?"

Bethany shook her head.

"How about fun food? What do you like to snack on?"

"I dunno. The other foster parents didn't let me snack."

Maria took in a sharp breath. "Well, that's not how we do things here! We definitely want you to snack when you're hungry. What do you like? Chips? Fruit? Chocolate?"

Bethany shrugged her shoulders again.

"Why don't you and Lisa head to the grocery store and you can pick out a few things? After all, a room doesn't really feel like home until you know your favorite foods are here!"

Lisa could see Bethany trying to decide how to answer. "Are you OK to walk around?"

"I... I'd rather sit."

"No worries. I tried to pick up some different things you might like." Lisa got up and went to the fridge. "You can write anything you want on this notepad." She opened the fridge, "Fruits and veggies... there's juice and milk here... and yogurt and fruit cups. I try to keep a couple different kinds of ice cream in the freezer, and there's some pizza poppers you can microwave whenever you want. I'll grab some dairy-free stuff the next time I'm shopping. Over here is the cupboard where most of the food is. Feel free to just snoop around until you find what you like!"

"It's OK. I can wait 'til meals."

Lisa sat back down at the table. "How many foster homes have you been in?"

"I dunno. Eight or nine."

"Geez. That's a lot of times to get to know a new place and new people."

Bethany nodded.

"I can't make you instantly feel comfortable. But I hope—we hope—that after a while it will feel OK here."

Again, Bethany nodded. After the constant chatter of Jaz and Alex, Lisa felt like she was carrying on a one-sided conversation. She looked at her mom for help.

"Well, I'm going to watch TV for a while before supper. Want to join me, Bethany?"

Bethany shrugged, and Maria wheeled herself to the living room. After a moment, the teen followed her, and tucked herself into the far corner of the couch. Lisa noticed her wince as she lifted her right foot up. Maria busied herself with transferring from her wheelchair to her specialized motorized recliner. Bethany watched her carefully, but didn't say anything.

Soon, the sounds of Maria's favorite home decorating show softened the awkwardness in the room. Lisa didn't know what to do. It was too early to start supper, and she didn't want Bethany to feel crowded by Lisa joining her on the couch. She got out her laptop and set it up at the table, making sure to angle herself so it didn't look like she was staring at their new houseguest. She wondered how long it would take for Bethany to start to feel comfortable.

After supper, Bethany carried her plate and cutlery to the counter. "Should I do the dishes?"

Lisa looked at her carefully. "I think you're having trouble standing up. Are you OK?"

"I'm fine."

"Well, maybe tomorrow you can help clean up. You've had a lot happening today, what with getting stuck with another set of foster people."

The relief on her face was obvious. "K, um, thanks." She turned and hobbled upstairs. Lisa looked back at her mom but knew what she would say. Hopefully, Bethany would tell them what was wrong when she was ready.

When Lisa went to bed that night, there wasn't any light coming from under Bethany's door. She wanted to check on her but decided not to disturb her in case she was sleeping.

CHAPTER 33

Bethany was sitting at the table when Lisa came down the next morning. She tried to hide her surprise that the teen was up early.

"Good morning! You must be hungry! Did you want some toast right away? I can't decide between pancakes and scrambled eggs this morning."

"Um, yeah. Toast? And scrambled eggs?"

"Perfect." She quickly put two pieces of bread in the toast and put a glass of juice in front of her. "You just sit there and watch me and you'll know where everything is in no time."

When everything was ready she put a plate in front of Bethany with everything at the table near her. "Help yourself, I'm just going to check on Mom." She hoped that a few moments alone to choose what to eat would help.

"Morning," she whispered as she opened her mom's bedroom door.

"Morning you! This is a nice way to start the morning!" Her mom sat propped up in bed, her computer on the hospital table in front of her, and her hand on the specially designed mouse that allowed her to navigate the internet without too much pain.

"I just wanted to give Bethany a moment to start eating without me there," Lisa said quietly.

"I'll join you in a bit. I just wanted to double check Jaz's schedule for the day. She's only got three appointments, which is good because it will take her a while to check the orders before they go out."

Maria still loved her work as an executive assistant for Jaz on the upcycling end of the Jazzy Clothing Company business. It was a lifeline for Jaz, and a way for Maria to still feel connected to everything.

"Do you want me to bring you your tea here?"

"No, I'm just about finished and then I won't be long before I join you."

Lisa was happy to see Bethany eating a full plate of food when she came back into the dining room.

"Is your mom OK?"

"Yep, she's just doing some early morning work. She'll be out in a minute." Lisa took a sip of her cooling coffee and helped herself to breakfast. Normally she finished her coffee long before making breakfast, but today was a day for being flexible. "So, I was thinking of bringing you to my friend who's a Physician's Assistant. She can do an initial check right away and then get you in to see the doctor when he's free."

"OK."

Lisa sent a text to Kara asking for her earliest appointment. All her friends were excited about her plan to foster older kids and were ready to help in any way they could. The news that a pregnant teenager would be living with her and Maria seemed to be a perfect fit.

"I can clean up so you can go to work."

"Oh, I work from home, so why don't we clean up together after Mom's done eating." She looked up as her mom wheeled herself into the dining room. "Wow, good timing!"

"Good morning Bethany! How did you sleep?"

"Good. Um, thanks... are you paralyzed?"

Maria and Lisa tried not to make eye contact. They had seen Jaz really gain confidence when she started asking questions. Hopefully, it would be the same for their newest family member. She explained about rheumatoid arthritis and how it impacted her day.

"Do you take pills for pain?"

"I do. Plus pills that keep inflammation down and others that slow the progress of the arthritis."

"Can I have a pain pill for my foot?"

"These ones would probably be a bad idea for your baby, but I'd like you to not be in so much pain. Do you know what's wrong? With your foot?"

"I dunno. It just really started hurting bad one day."

Maria gasped, "Oh my dear! That's terrible! What did the doctor say?"

"I didn't go to a doctor."

"We'll be sure to tell Kara about it," Lisa promised.

"When are you going to see her?" Maria turned to Bethany, "You'll love Kara!"

Lisa looked down at her buzzing phone. "10:30 today!"

"Well, that's good news. You know Bethany, if it wasn't for Kara we probably wouldn't be here! A few years ago, Lisa and I had just reconnected for the first time after she left home. I was really sick, and Lisa got an appointment with Kara to talk about it. She was trying so hard to take care of me, and Kara put her in contact with another friend of hers who grew up caring for a mom in a wheel-chair. That other friend is Carrie—you'll love her too!"

Maria smiled as she talked about the people in her life. "Anyway, Carrie's a counselor, and she helped us get our heads on straight and deal with all the changes that were happening. And then she intro-duced us to more people who are all really good friends now!"

Lisa took over the story, "Kara's also the one who took Jaz—the girl who lived here until a few months ago with her baby boy—over to Carrie's when Jaz got kicked out of her home for being pregnant. And then Jaz moved in here a little while later."

Bethany looked from Maria to Lisa, "Are you, like, a pregnant girls' charity or something?"

"Mom and I got a second chance at pretty much everything after a really rough start. We were never close when I was younger, and I took off after graduation to get away from my dad. Now that we can be together, and we don't have an abusive man in our life anymore we keep trying to help others. It's not about pregnant girls, really. Just that we have this house, and we both want to give others the second chance that we've had."

"Oh. My second chance got wrecked a long time ago."

"Not with us," Maria insisted.

The doorbell rang, and Lisa went to answer it. Mark stood there with a grocery bag holding a laptop. "Here it is! It should work OK, but let me know if it doesn't." Lisa accepted the bag and he turned around and jogged back to the car. She could see two children sitting in the back seat.

"I don't know if this is good news or bad news for you," she said as she came back into the dining room, "but your laptop is here so you can start school!"

"Oh, this is exciting! What grade are you in?"

Bethany paused. "Um, nine I think? I kinda haven't been at school for a while."

"Well, I can help you with anything with numbers. But I'm not very good at anything with reading."

"I love reading, so I can help with that." Maria offered. "If you want, of course."

"I don't know if it will be hard."

"Let's get this stuff cleaned up and then we'll find out." Lisa stood up, and Bethany followed her lead. In a short time, everything was cleaned up, and the table had everyone's laptops on it. Lisa found Bethany's laptop agonizingly slow, but eventually they were on the online school site.

"Huh, it looks like you can choose any class to start, and do as much as you want at a time. That's kinda cool!" Lisa thought back to her time finishing her bookkeeping certificate. She would never have managed online courses.

When it was time to leave for the doctor's appointment, Bethany looked up in surprise. "That went so fast!"

Lisa hoped it was a sign that the online schooling would work out for her. "We can leave everything out on the table."

"Can't I bring it with me?"

"You can, but you probably won't have internet access while we're out."

"Oh, right."

"We'll have to go on a working coffee run sometime," Lisa promised. "Then we can hook up to the internet at the coffee shop and work there. It's one of my favorite things to do."

Bethany's eyes lit up. "Really? Cool!"

"Definitely. I always get a lot done when I do that."

During the drive Lisa tried to prepare her for the appointment. "So, like I said, today you'll be seeing Kara, and then we'll make the appointment to see the doctor. You can ask her anything—about your pregnancy, your health, babies…"

Bethany looked out the side window and didn't answer. Lisa knew she couldn't force her to talk, but it would be a lot easier if she knew what she was going through.

CHAPTER 34

"I can't believe it!" Maria exclaimed, "You've had a huge sliver in your foot for weeks?"

Bethany smiled, "Well, it's not like I could see it. My stomach got in the way!"

Lisa shuddered at the memory. Kara came out to the reception area to get Lisa to sit with Bethany while they removed the sliver. She only let herself have a tiny glance at Bethany's heel, but the image of the flaming red, swollen heel would be stuck in her mind for a while. Now they needed to keep a close eye on it to make sure the infection didn't spread. Bethany still hobbled when she walked, but said the pain was less already.

"Kara said another day or two and Bethany would have been in the hospital on IV antibiotics!"

"Sounds like everything worked out then. And what do you know about your baby and the due date?"

"Um, the baby has a really loud heartbeat. Kara let me listen! And she said I'll probably have the baby in April." For the first time since she arrived, her hand smoothed her shirt over her stomach affectionately.

"Aha!" Lisa exclaimed. "There's a prenatal class starting next week in the same building as Mom's exercise class, almost at the same time." She looked up from her phone. "Would you like to go?"

"Can you come with me?"

"Of course! It starts half an hour after the exercise classes, so we'll just hang out and then I'll go in with you. I haven't had any babies of my own, but this is my second round of prenatal classes, so I'm practically an expert!" she joked.

"And, um… I wanted to take a bath. Is that OK?" On Kara's advice, they had stopped at the drugstore and picked up a special cover that would keep Bethany's bandaged foot dry until it healed. Lisa didn't want to push bathing, but Kara just came right out and told Bethany to make sure she was having a bath or shower every other day.

"Any time you want. That's your bathroom now. Did you want to wash any clothes at the same time? I have this special hot water tank thing so we can run anything in the house at the same time and you won't run out of hot water."

"I only have the one set of clothes… but maybe I could wash my extra socks and underwear?"

There was silence for a minute. Maria recovered first. "There should be a robe hanging in the closet. Why don't you put that on so we can run a load with everything? I can switch it over to the dryer for you —that's actually one thing I can do on my own, and it's nice to be able to help. And then I have a silly gift card to a department store that I'll never use. Why don't we send Lisa over there to pick up some basics for you? Once your foot feels better we'll have some fun shopping for you, but for now you need more than one set of clothes."

Bethany looked from Lisa to Maria slowly, and then down at the floor. "I can't pay you back," she mumbled. "But thanks anyways."

"I can't imagine what you're feeling, or what you've gone through. But we're here for you. Like really good friends, or maybe one day we'll even feel like family to you. It takes time for that to happen, and Mom and I are patient. But we *want* to make you feel a little more comfortable now. Today. It's a gift to help you out. No strings attached, and no debts. And if you have to leave, everything that's yours will still be yours to keep. Can you live with that?"

Bethany nodded without looking up.

"Great! I'll head out then. Are there any colors you hate or love? Or things you need?"

Bethany shook her head. Lisa quickly got ready for shopping and slipped out the door. She wanted to get Bethany in some new, clean clothes as soon as possible, and she trusted her mom to make Bethany feel a little more at ease.

When she was out she texted Jaz:

> *First foster girl is settling in. Her name's Bethany and she's about 7 months pregnant. I'm just off to get some basics, since she only came with one set of clothes.*

Jaz replied almost immediately:

> *Yay! You guys are perfect for this! I can't wait to meet her and design some cool clothes. How about we come over for supper tonight?*

Lisa laughed. Jaz's plan to have her mom do her cooking wasn't working out yet. She was probably getting tired of eating takeout.

> *For sure! I'm making stirfry. But you're not coming for the food...right?*

> *Are you kidding? I'm definitely coming for the food! LOL!*

At the department store she bought some loose maternity shirts, soft leggings, socks, underwear, a nightgown, and a warm hoodie. It was enough to get by, and they could always donate anything that didn't work to the thrift store.

Back at home, Bethany sat on the couch in her robe, watching TV with Maria. With no makeup on and with her hair hanging damp, she barely looked 15. Lisa knew her childhood was officially over, and maybe had been for a long time. Things would be hard, but not impossible. And maybe visiting with Jaz tonight would inspire her to start looking forward to the future.

"Hey you two! I'm just going to pop these clothes in the washer and then I'll come join you. Mom, do you need anything?"

Maria looked up from her recliner. "I'd love a hot chocolate and one of those gingerbread cookies we bought from the bakery."

"Sure! Sound good for you too Bethany?"

"I don't think I like gingerbread. Can I maybe have toast?"

"Of course! I'll bring it over in a few minutes. Just so you know, I'm going to keep doing this kind of stuff for you until your foot's better. I know you're perfectly capable of getting your own snacks, but for now you need to stay off your foot as much as possible, OK?"

Bethany nodded, and Lisa went to the laundry room. The old clothes were already dry, but Lisa wanted her in something new. Saying a little 'thank you' to herself for the machine that could run a quick load, she started the wash, put the clothes from the dryer into a basket, and then went to get snacks and drinks for everyone.

"So," she said as she settled onto the couch, "Jaz and Alex are coming over for supper tonight. We mentioned her already."

Bethany nodded.

They watched TV in silence until the buzzer went for the washing machine. Lisa got up to switch over the laundry and start supper.

Normally she and her mom had a running conversation going when she cooked, but today it felt a little hard to do that. When the dryer buzzed Lisa carried the laundry upstairs with Bethany walking carefully behind. Once in her room, she didn't come out.

Jaz's arrival brought the energy and noise that Lisa and Maria were missing. Alex immediately reached out for Lisa, and she picked him up for cuddles before helping take his winter clothes off.

"Hey you! Are you missing Aunty Lisa?"

He answered with "Da!"

"I think that means yes," Jaz said, "but it could also mean more, stop, and no."

They all laughed, and Alex looked delighted with the attention.

"Now that you've got him, I'm going to run out and get a bag of clothes. Where's my new bestie?"

"She's upstairs in her room. I'll go get her." Lisa walked upstairs still holding Alex and knocked quietly on the door.

"Yeah?"

"Jaz and Alex are here. Are you OK to come down?"

"Oh, yeah sure. In a sec."

Lisa wondered what Bethany did in her room with no phone, TV, or computer. *If she's going to hang out up there all the time I should get her a TV or something.*

Bethany came down looking like she was going to an execution, but Jaz didn't seem to notice. "Hi, I'm Jaz, and this is my baby Alex. Oh my gosh! I love your hair! And you're the perfect size! Here, let's go into the living room, I think I have some maternity clothes that will fit you."

The two girls went into the living room, and Jaz immediately started pulling things out of a large bag.

"OK, you're definitely more urban trendy than I was. So button-up dresses aren't your thing. But what about these shirts? This one says 'Mama' in Greek, and here's the matching little shirt that says 'baby' so you two can be all cute and matching. I've sold a *ton* of these!"

Bethany ran her hand over the lettering on the baby shirt for a second before Alex crawled over and sat right on it. He looked at her expectantly, and Bethany stared back. After a minute Alex moved on to Lisa and Maria, where he got the immediate attention he was used to.

By the time supper was on the table Bethany had a variety of custom maternity clothes that she could wear.

Dinner was a lot more relaxed with Jaz's talking and Alex's chatter and antics. Bethany watched him carefully, but didn't make any effort to interact with him.

"So," Jaz said turning to her, "What are you hoping for? A boy or a girl?"

"Girl."

"Do you have any names picked out?"

"No."

"Did you get sick at first? I had the *worst* morning sickness! That was how my mom found out I was pregnant!"

"Um, yeah. I was kinda sick. The people I stayed with then made me go to school. I'd just hang out in the handicapped bathroom."

"Geez. That sucks. My parents kicked me out and ghosted me until Alex was, like, two months old. But then Maria found my mom and convinced her to change her mind. Now my parents can't get enough of Alex!"

Bethany lifted her head and looked at Maria, "Do you think you could find my mom?"

"Well, Jaz didn't tell the part where I literally fell over myself, broke my ankle, and ended up getting x-rayed by her mom. I just happened to realize who she was, and started talking about Jaz and Alex. But I'd be happy to try anything to help you. When did you last hear from her?"

"Like, five months ago. She texted me that she was in town and wanted me to meet her at the bus station. I went, but she wasn't there anymore. And then my foster parents took my cell phone away."

"Doesn't Mark have your parent's details?"

"No, it was a different agency when I got taken away. They told him they never had my mom's info but that's a total lie. He let me use his phone to try and call her, but it always goes to voicemail."

"I don't know what else we can do, but you're welcome to borrow my phone after supper to try to call her. Do you know the name of the place where she works, or any of her friends or anything?"

"No, my mom's kind of a loner. That's why I need to find her. I know how to get her to talk and stuff."

"Well, I sure hope you can find her. Lisa and I are proof that you can reconnect with family no matter how long you've been apart."

"I am too!" Jaz reminded her. "I had given up hope of having a relationship with my parents, but things are really good now!"

"I'll bet they're happy about Alex starting Mandarin daycare!"

"Totally! Now that I'm behaving like a proper daughter again, they can brag about me."

"Jaz's parents wanted her to become a doctor," Lisa explained to Bethany, "And they were pretty upset when they found out she wouldn't go to university like they planned for her. But she's built this huge clothing company, and it's so successful her dad is working for her now! So they've gotten over the whole university thing."

"Well, not exactly. My mom likes to remind me that it's never too late to go back to school. But I try not to pay attention to that. She's good to Alex, and I can't wait until she retires and they can help out more."

CHAPTER 35

A week later, Mark came by to see how things were going. Again, they sat at the table, but now Lisa brought over flavored sparkling water for Bethany. It wasn't Diet Coke, which was what she wanted, but at least it was fizzy. The refusal to buy Diet Coke brought on the only tension between Lisa and Bethany, but Lisa refused to let her drink it while she was pregnant unless she bought it for herself.

"So, how's your foot doing?" Mark asked as soon as he sat down.

"Good. Kara—she's the person at the doctor's—said it's all good now."

"I apologize for that. I went and insisted the foster family show me the room you were staying in. That floor was an absolute hazard, and I missed it when I did the inspection. There's no excuse for that and I've withdrawn their names from our list."

"Yeah, they sucked."

"So, what are things like here?"

"Good." She smiled at Lisa. "They're nice. I like my room."

"I'd like to see it before I go if that's OK."

"Yeah."

"And how's the online school going?"

"It's good. I think I can maybe finish ninth grade before the baby comes."

"Bethany! That's fantastic! Way to go!" He lifted his hand for a high five, and she half-heartedly gave him one.

"And Lisa, how do you think things are going?"

"Good! Bethany's pretty quiet. It's nice to have her here, and now that she can walk more easily she's really helping out. After breakfast, mom and I work while she does her school, except for the morning when she has prenatal class."

"What's that like for you?" he looked at Bethany.

She shrugged, "The other women kinda stare at me, but Lisa acts like nothing's wrong."

"So Lisa's going to be your birthing coach?"

"Yeah. She helped her friend Jaz do it, so she already knows stuff."

"And how are you set up for when baby comes?"

Bethany looked at Lisa, who answered, "We've got everything from when Jaz and Alex lived here. All Bethany needs now are things like diapers, wipes, and maybe formula."

"Definitely formula. I'm not doing that other thing."

"OK, well, Lisa will pay for those things initially, and then get reimbursed for them." He turned to Lisa, "Make sure you keep all your receipts."

She nodded. Bethany asked about another foster child who had been in care with her. As she and Mark talked, Lisa's mind wandered. Things were OK for now, but what would happen in the years to come? How would Bethany be able to support herself and a child? Lisa knew that all foster support ended when the child in care turned

18. But what skills would she have then? Would it be enough? It seemed like a nearly impossible situation.

"What?" Mark had asked her a question.

He smiled, "Just wondering if you knew anything about all the construction happening around our office. I know you were pretty vocal about how inaccessible it was. And now the property owner is making a big show about how he's using his own money to make everything accessible."

"Really? Yeah, I totally harassed him and his entire company! And then I kinda forgot about it all when Bethany came. Well, I'm really glad he's taking action now. And your clients will have a much easier time when they can get in the door with a stroller or a wheelchair!"

"Well, we all want to thank you for what you did. The other businesses are really going to benefit when everything's done. And you're right, it'll make our office feel more welcoming to everyone who visits."

He finished his coffee and stood up, "I guess the only thing that's left is to make sure you're not sleeping in a room with bare boards on the floor!"

"Oh, yeah." Bethany got up and walked towards the stairs and Mark followed her. Lisa waited downstairs. She was shocked the property owner had fixed the entrances. While it was important, it couldn't come cheap. But he was doing the right thing. She put a reminder in her phone to call and thank him.

After Mark checked the bedroom, he said a quick good-bye and headed out. Bethany stayed upstairs. Lisa put up a small flat screen TV a few days ago. She hoped she was giving Bethany a nice way to stay entertained, and not a reason to hide away all day. With Jaz she had felt much more like they were friends, but with Bethany she felt like more of a parent. The only problem was that she had no idea how to parent a quiet, pregnant 15-year-old who only lit up when she talked about finding her mom.

She got out her laptop and set up to work. With the extra appointments and shopping for Bethany she got a lot less done than she used to. It was good to be busy, but she questioned whether they were really making a difference for her. She always said thank you, but she never volunteered information or asked questions about anything except borrowing a phone. At least she was safe, clean, and taken care of but it didn't feel like enough.

When Lisa finished her work, she went to see her mom. Maria was taking a day to rest in bed after feeling a bit under the weather. It wasn't much of anything, but they both knew that rest was the best defense against winter illnesses. Once March was over in a few weeks the risk of getting the flu would hopefully go down.

That night when Bethany made her usual attempt at calling her mom, someone answered the phone. They were all shocked, and it took Bethany a moment to be able to talk. "I'm looking for my mom. Her name's Esther Palmer. This is her number... Can you tell her Bethany called? And give her this number? It's— oh. OK. Bye"

She returned the phone to Maria. "I think that was her new boyfriend. I hope he's nice. He said he'd pass on the message."

"Oh Bethany, that would be wonderful!"

"Yeah. I'm, um, I'm gonna go do some more school upstairs. Night."

"Night," they both answered.

"Do you think she's OK?" Lisa asked quietly.

"I have no idea. We'll just have to keep trying to be there for her. Maybe when she's back with her mother everything will sort itself out."

"I hope so."

For the next few days, Bethany seemed more intent than ever on finishing ninth grade. She often took the laptop to her room, and Lisa could see the blue glow from a screen shining under the bedroom door when she went to bed.

"Can I take Tylenol?" Bethany asked after pushing away her morning toast. "My back is killing me!"

"Maybe you need a desk to work at in your room. But yeah, I'll grab you a Tylenol."

They cleaned up breakfast as usual, and all the ladies settled in with their laptops, but it wasn't long before Bethany leaned back in her chair and groaned. "Geez! This sucks!"

"Is there any chance you're in labor?" Maria asked.

They all looked at each other. "It's not supposed to be 'til April!"

"Well, they said the baby will come whenever it's ready. Is your hospital bag packed?" Lisa tried to get Bethany to choose what she wanted to bring to the hospital but eventually went on her own and shopped off a checklist she found online.

"No," she grunted, "Maybe I'll just go pack now." She grabbed her laptop and charger.

"Oh, you don't have to bring those! Take a few days off of school, you've earned it!"

"It's OK. I really want to get my stuff done." She walked awkwardly towards the stairs with her free hand rubbing her lower back.

Lisa quickly finished what she was doing and saved it. Closing her laptop she smiled at her mom. "I guess we'll be enjoying the sounds of a newborn soon!"

"I'm so excited!"

"Yeah, you get to hang out here and wait for good news. You should be excited!"

"I'll send out a group email to everyone once we know for sure she's in labor. I'm sure they'll all want to know."

It wasn't until almost a day later that Bethany's labor progressed to the point that Maria could send out her email. In that time Lisa took her to the hospital, waited for hours, got sent home, and then headed back out again a few hours later.

"If they don't think you're ready yet, we can just wait in the waiting room." she promised. Bethany acted angry about being sent home, but Lisa suspected she was really more afraid about what was coming and didn't want to show it.

When they got into a labor room Lisa did everything in her power to make Bethany more comfortable, but nothing helped. She was in agony, afraid, and lashing out at everyone who tried to help. It was a side of her that surprised Lisa, and she took frequent breaks to step outside the room and compose herself.

"Just be glad you're not the father!" one of the nurses joked. "We've seen some pretty powerful stuff coming at them over the years!"

Lisa tried to give her a smile, "Thanks."

When the first cry from a five pound, six ounce baby boy filled the room, Lisa found tears streaming down her face. "You did it!" she told Bethany. "You have a perfect, gorgeous baby boy!"

Bethany's face didn't change, even when he was placed in her arms. She seemed detached as she looked down on him.

"Give her some time," the nurse whispered to Lisa, "It's quite a shock for the young ones."

Lisa quietly stepped out and called her mom. "It's a boy! But Bethany doesn't seem very happy."

"Give her some time."

"That's exactly what the nurse said! Well, at least they're both OK. I'm so exhausted. I can't imagine what Bethany's feeling!"

She sat down on a chair right outside the delivery room and rested her head on her hand.

"Lisa?" A nurse squatted beside her patting her on the arm. "You can go in now!"

"Oh, thanks!" She walked in to see Bethany almost asleep, with the baby in a bassinet right beside her. "Hey!" she said quietly.

Bethany smiled shakily, "I'm glad that's over."

"No kidding. Congratulations!"

"Thanks!"

"Can I get you anything?"

"A Diet Coke?"

Lisa paused.

"I'm not breastfeeding him no matter what. And I'm dying for a Diet Coke."

"Alight, you kinda deserve it after the last 24 hours! Anything else?"

"Maybe, like, can you get two cans so I can have one later? And, some food that's packaged? You know, so I can eat it whenever I get hungry."

"Of course! I think there's a kitchen here too that will have some stuff you can help yourself to whenever, just ask the nurse."

"OK, cool."

It took Lisa longer than she expected to find a vending machine that sold Diet Coke, and then she went to the cafeteria and bought some granola bars, cheese strings, and mini boxes of dry cereal. Even after spending almost two months with Bethany she still didn't know what she preferred to eat.

When she got back to the room, Bethany was sound asleep. Lisa left the food on the bedside table and watched the baby sleeping for a minute. He looked so peaceful and vulnerable. She said a little prayer for him and went home to get some much-needed sleep.

CHAPTER 36

"Lisa?" Maria called from downstairs.

Lisa opened her eyes and struggled to remember what day it was. She looked at her alarm clock. 10:33. She had never slept so late!

"Lisa?"

"Hang on!"

Lisa got up and put her robe on before going downstairs. It was chilly for near the end of March. Definitely time for spring weather to come!

Mark stood at the front door, with her mom still holding the door handle. Lisa had left him a voicemail the day before about Bethany having a healthy baby boy.

"Mark! What's up?"

"Do you know if Bethany came back here last night?"

"Are you kidding? She just had a baby yesterday!"

"She's gone."

"What? With the baby?"

"No. Can you just check upstairs in case she's here, or she came by to get her things?"

Lisa ran up the stairs and opened the bedroom door. Everything was neat and tidy. Too neat and tidy compared to how the room usually was. She walked in and then looked in the bathroom. There was a note propped up on the counter.

> *Dear Lisa,*
> *You're a good person. I'm not. Take care of the baby. It needs*
> *a mom.*
> *Thanks for being nice to me.*
> *Bethany*

She stood there for a few minutes, trying to come to grips with what the note meant.

"Lisa?" There was a quiet knock at the bedroom door.

She picked up the note and walked out. Wordlessly she handed it to Mark.

He sighed.

"What happens now?" Lisa asked.

"The hospital can keep the baby for a few days while I try to find a foster family. Newborns are hard to place though." He looked up from the note. "Did she give you any idea she was thinking of running?"

Lisa shook her head. "She's been working super hard on school. And she got through to that number the other day and left a message for her mom…"

"Maybe she found her. But I have to admit, I didn't expect this."

Lisa pictured the helpless newborn, now alone in the hospital. It was unbearable to think of him not having anyone to love him. She looked over to the extra room where everything for a baby was ready.

"Can I keep him? Until Bethany comes back? I mean, I'm not an expert on babies, but I did help Jaz out when she had Alex. And I've got lots of support from friends."

"Would you? That would be just amazing Lisa. Especially since you're already approved as a foster parent. But I have to warn you, Bethany may never come back."

"Of course she will! She's just scared right now. Give her some time. That's what everyone else told me about her. Give her some time. And then she'll know where her baby is. Did she name him?"

"Not that I know of. Well, let's go see how your mom feels about caring for a baby."

"I heard." Maria called up to them as they walked down the stairs. "And of course we'll keep the little one until his mommy's ready for him. The poor girl. Won't she need medical care?"

"Well, the nurses said she would have been released this morning."

"I can't believe I slept in! I should have been there this morning."

"Lisa, one thing I can tell you for sure is that you could not have prevented this. Foster kids—all kids for that matter—make their own choices about life. Nothing you could have done would have prevented Bethany from leaving when she decided to."

"I have a hard time believing you, but regardless, I need to get to the hospital." She paused, "What do we call him?"

"That's up to you. I don't even know what my legal requirements are when I have a baby in care with no name. You have an infant car seat?"

"Yep, from Jaz. We have everything except a mom."

"You're wrong. A foster mom is as much a mom as a birth mom. This little guy will know love wherever it comes from. But I'll need a few hours to make sure all the paperwork is properly in place. Fortunately, I set him up in the system as under your care already, so it shouldn't be too long. Do you want to wait here and I'll call you when things are ready?"

"No. I'll grab a quick shower and something to eat, but I want to be there with him. Even if there's a wait, at least he won't be alone."

He placed his hand on Lisa's shoulder, "Bethany got one part of that note right. You *are* a good person. Thank you for being willing to take care of this little guy."

"You're welcome."

She stood still for a minute after Mark closed the door behind him. "You ready for this?" she asked her mom.

"All I know is that that little boy belongs here for as long as necessary. The rest will sort itself out. You go get ready and I'll update everyone on the new circumstances."

CHAPTER 37

Lisa walked into the hospital carrying an empty car seat. It felt surreal to think that she'd soon be leaving with a baby.

When she got to the nursery, the nurses all greeted her warmly. "We've been calling him baby Palmer. The social worker called and said to let you pick a name."

"I wish Bethany told me something—anything! All I know is that she wanted a girl… What about Marcus? You know, kind of after the social worker, Mark?"

"I think he looks like a Marcus! Now, come on in and we'll get you settled while you wait for the paperwork. Baby Marcus has just been fed, but he could use some cuddles."

The nurse pointed Lisa towards a rocking chair, and a swaddled baby was placed in her arms. She looked down into big blue eyes. "Hey little guy! I guess I'm your stand-in mommy. Your mommy's out there somewhere. I know she's thinking about you. And one day she's going to want to meet you! So I'll take really good care of you until she comes back, OK?"

His eyes slowly closed and Lisa began to memorize every feature of his face. After a while she lifted her head up and looked around the nursery. A few parents came to pick up babies and there was a peaceful feeling in the room. She remembered from Alex's delivery that most parents kept their babies with them until they left the hospital.

Beside the bassinet where the nurse picked up Marcus she saw the diaper bag they brought. Like the hospital bag, Lisa had ended up buying the things on her own. Bethany had no interest in any baby shopping. Had it always been her plan to leave right after delivering her baby?

The same nurse came in. "Everything's set for you to take Marcus home. Mark sent his apologies, he wanted to see you off from the hospital but he's had an emergency come up with one of his other charges. Do you need us to go over anything before you leave?"

"Oh, yeah. I need to know about when I feed him and how much."

"Of course. I'll write it down for you."

Half an hour later Lisa was walking down the hallway carrying the diaper bag, and the car seat with Marcus safely strapped in. She had a moment of wondering if she was doing the right thing, and debated turning around. She couldn't care for a newborn! But then she remembered Mark talking about it being difficult to find a foster home. Surely she could handle this. And one day Bethany *would* come back. Of that she was certain. So she kept walking.

In the elevator, an elderly couple cooed over the baby. "You look lovely for just giving birth!" the woman said. "You women these days are just amazing!"

Lisa almost corrected her, before smiling her thanks. She didn't trust herself to say anything. As she walked towards her car with her new foster son, she felt like she was standing at a distance watching herself.

This was nothing she had ever considered. In all her ideas about what to do with her life, and how to meet the undefined longing in her heart to love someone, she had never dreamed of walking out of a hospital with a newborn baby.

She tripled checked to make sure the car seat was secure before driving below the speed limit the entire way home. It was so quiet in the car. Was Marcus OK? Maybe he couldn't breathe or something. She signaled to pull over and then heard him begin to cry. With a sigh of relief, she turned off her signal and kept driving. By the time she pulled into the driveway Marcus was effectively exercising his right to express himself.

"Sounds like he's figured out a few things already! Oh my, Lisa, he's so beautiful!"

Lisa set the car seat on the floor so she could take off her shoes and coat. Marcus continued to wail. "The nurse gave me a feeding schedule but I couldn't care less about it! This little guy is getting a bottle whether the time is right or not."

"Atta girl!" Maria smiled, "You're already doing great!"

"Why don't you come to the living room, and you can hold him while I get the formula made? They gave me some pre-sterilized bottles, so I shouldn't be too long."

Lisa had already prepared water for Bethany to use to make formula so she quickly made up a bottle. Her mom looked down at Marcus and with one of the biggest smiles Lisa had ever seen. She reluctantly took him from her and settled on the couch. It only took a few tries for him to latch on and start sucking.

"I'm so conflicted!" Maria said. "I'm just heartbroken over Bethany not being here for these moments and wondering if she's OK. And at the same time we've got this perfect little baby that we can give all our love to. More than we could have if she was here!"

Lisa nodded in agreement, "Yeah, that's exactly it. Mom, it felt so weird walking out of the hospital with a baby and knowing everyone thought he was mine."

"He *is* yours, Lisa. You have to think of it that way. At least for today he's yours, and that's all we can think about."

"Well, for the first time in my life I don't feel like I'm missing out on anything. It's like I have it all right here. You're right, it may not be forever, but we'll give this little guy the best start he can possibly have."

A gentle knock sounded at the door. "Oh, I'll bet that's Carrie. I'll be right back." Maria turned and wheeled herself to the entryway.

The sound of quiet voices came from the entrance, and then Carrie, Jonathan, Matthew, and Katie all walked in.

"Hey guys! Come on over and meet Marcus Palmer. He's had a good round of vocal exercise while he waited for his bottle, and now he's ready to meet all of you."

They all crowded around, and Lisa felt tears filling her eyes.

Carrie sat down and put an arm around her, "Hey, you are exactly where you're meant to be right now, and so is this little guy."

Lisa smiled, "I think you're right."

"And wherever this journey takes you, we will support you and help you in any way you need."

"And when he's bigger I can play with him, just like I play with Brittany and Alex!" added Katie, hopping from one foot to the other.

"I think he'll like that Katie! Thank you!"

Maria wheeled over with a box from the bakery in her lap, "Here you go, everyone help yourself to some baking!"

They all crowded around her to choose, and Lisa soaked in the image of her mom, completely happy, surrounded by people who loved her. Somehow her life kept taking the most bizarre and unexpected turns, and every time, the surprise around the corner was better than she could have ever imagined.

She felt Marcus lose his connection on the bottle, and she carefully set him on her shoulder to burp him. He obliged almost immediately.

"Alright, as soon as you're ready we can play pass the baby." While they finished eating, she stroked the feathery halo of hair on Marcus' head, then put her phone on the bookshelf behind them and set the camera to record the happy hubbub around them. She'd take lots of pictures and videos of him so when Bethany came back, she would have a record of every important moment and milestone.

Just a few miles away, Bethany shifted uncomfortably. Why did bus seats have to be so hard? Everything hurt. Her body and her heart. It took her longer to leave the hospital than she expected. Did everyone fall in love with their babies so fast?

She shook her head and angrily brushed away the tears that kept falling down her cheeks. Her mom needed her now, and she couldn't take care of her mom *and* a baby. Plus, Mark had carefully explained to her how Lisa would be legally responsible for her baby. So he wasn't really hers, was he?

Opening the grocery bag she'd pulled out of the garbage at the hospital, she looked at the few items she could call 'hers'. There were the snacks Lisa left at her bedside. Some gross oversized pads that were stocked in the hospital bathroom. And a handful of change—all the money she had left after begging for money and buying a one-way bus ticket. Her mom promised she had enough money for a hotel room when Bethany got to her. Everything would be fine then. She'd get a job, and help her mom quit drinking. This time would be different.

Lisa reached out with her cell phone in her hand. It took a little bit of work to get it angled so it caught her face and Marcus sleeping in her arms. Tomorrow she'd buy a selfie stick so she could take videos more easily. With a tap of her thumb, the red 'recording' light turned on.

"Hey Bethany. Here we are. Um, as you can see, your son is sound asleep. He's had a full first day. Carrie and Jonathan and the kids stopped over to see him, and he was always in someone's arms…

"We're calling him Marcus. Kind of a nod to Mark, the social worker. I hope that's OK. I wish I knew what you wanted to name him." Lisa paused, and tried not to get too emotional, "I hope you're OK. I can't imagine what you're going through right now. If I could I'd send you a message to let you know that we're here for you, and you've got a gorgeous, healthy son."

She looked down at Marcus and smiled, "He's got your eyes. The shape of them. And he's got a really good set of lungs, too! Anyways, I hope you find what you're looking for. And Marcus, Mom, and I will be here. Whenever you want to come home. I don't know. Maybe this never felt like home to you. I wanted it to, but…

"Well, wherever you are now, whatever's going on… we're here for you. I'll do my best to take care of Marcus. I guess I'll be finding out what it's like to lose sleep every night… I hope you have somewhere safe to sleep tonight. Bye for now."

She turned off her phone and set it on the little table beside the armchair in her bedroom. The bassinet stood beside her bed now. And she had carried the change table into her bathroom. There had always been more room than she needed. Lots of extra room for a baby and all his things.

Carefully, she got up and laid Marcus down in his own little bed. He fussed for a few seconds, but never woke up. She walked downstairs and peeked into her mom's room. She had fallen asleep with her light on. Lisa quietly took the novel out of her mom's hand where it was still open and laid it to the side before turning out the light and leaving the room.

She checked that the doors and windows were locked, and then poured herself a glass of wine and sat at the table. In some ways, the future was even more uncertain now. Bethany could show up at any time, or maybe some other relative who would want Marcus. At least she *thought* that could happen. Could it? Maybe Mark would know.

But right now—for tonight at least—everything was peaceful and settled. She felt overwhelmed and fulfilled in a way she never imagined. It took a few minutes for her to realize she was sitting in the half-dark, smiling to herself. *You're being really weird, Lisa.* She took her empty wine glass to the sink and rinsed it out. Her reflection shone vaguely back at her from the kitchen window. *Not weird. Happy. Content.*

With a smile still on her face, she walked upstairs to get whatever sleep she could before Marcus woke up.

A NOTE FROM THE AUTHOR

Thank you for taking the time to read *A Lifetime of Love*! If you enjoyed it, please consider telling your friends or posting a short review. Word of mouth is an author's best friend and much appreciated! Thank you again!

To be one of the first to hear when my next book comes out, and for a chance to win bookish prizes, sign-up for my newsletter:

www.carmenklassen.com

You can also follow me on Facebook:

fb.me/CarmenKlassen.Author

May all your days be full of good books, nice people, and happy endings.

Sincerely,

Carmen

ALSO BY CARMEN KLASSEN

SUCCESS ON HER TERMS SERIES

Book 1: Sweet, Smart, and Struggling

Book 2: The Cost of Caring

Book 3: Life Upcycled

Book 4: Heartwarming Designs

Book 5: A Roof Over Their Heads

Book 6: A Lifetime of Love

* * *

NON-FICTION TITLES

Love Your Clutter Away

Before Your Parents Move In

Manufactured by Amazon.ca
Bolton, ON